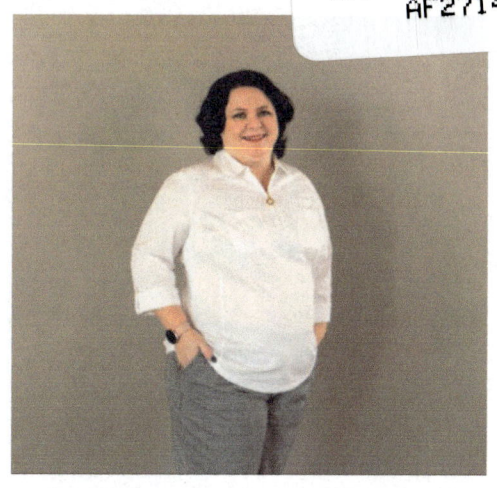

About the Author

Dina Wecker is an educator with a passion for reading and writing. She has an Ed.S. degree in early literacy and spends her free time reading and reviewing books for readers of all ages. She lives with her husband, two children, and dog in beautiful, Salt Lake City, Utah.

CONCEPTION

Dina Wecker

CONCEPTION

Vanguard Press

A CIP catalogue record for this title is
available from the British Library.

ISBN 978 1 80016 712 4

Vanguard Press is an imprint of
Pegasus Elliot Mackenzie Publishers Ltd.
www.pegasuspublishers.com

First Published in **2023**

Vanguard Press
Sheraton House Castle Park
Cambridge England

Printed & Bound in Great Britain

Dedication

To my daughter, that she never go through what her foremothers had to in order to just be herself.

Acknowledgements

Thank you to all of my trauma, generational and personal, for challenging me to become more than I ever dreamed. And for therapy for giving me the tools to get there. Above everything else, for a healthy, loving relationship with boundaries and support to do all the things I only dared whisper about in the dark.

Day 1
Brick

The windows on my Subaru rental are rolled down and the warm air floods in and blows my papers on the seat beside me in tiny circles around the car. The desert smells hot and slightly rotted. I smooth the map again and look for the name of the streets before Juniper Hill Court where I am meant to turn left. I take a quick sip from the green smoothie and slow to read each road name as I pass. I begin to see the names of trees and know that I am coming close: Sage Crest, Spruce Top, Sandalwood Cove, finally Juniper Hill Court, and I turn, slowing the car to an almost stop. I fluff my red curls around my face and shoulders and re-apply a layer of powder and Burt's Bee's Lip Gloss. I am wearing a skirt made from up-cycled floral prints and a fitted T-shirt that reads: 'Keep It Green'. My orange flowered Chacos and amber necklace top off the ensemble. I fidget with the skirt band, not having worn this skirt in nearly 8 years, and it isn't really as snug as it is awkward. It fits, but it is not as comfortable as I remember.

One more look in the rear-view mirror and I notice my wild eyes. Blue and fiery. I take a small bottle out of my patchwork purse and dab a Lavender mixture on my neck and inhale deeply. "Calm... calm... calm..." I tell myself and sit until I can feel my heart rate decreasing and my mind letting go of all the things that could go wrong, "Just be in the moment," I remind myself and begin to look at the small numbers on the white, orange, or yellow stucco houses.

913 Juniper Hill Court. I park my car on the curb, not the driveway, and get right out of the car. No pep talks, no time for waiting or hesitation... "You've come this far," I tell myself as I slam the car door shut. The green sporty Legacy looks nothing like my rusting green Outback wagon with bumper stickers and Chinese wealth charms hanging from the mirror, but I can still see a similar spirit between this car and mine. They were family and if I was broken down on some vista in the desert in my car, the owner of this one would feel some sort of kinship and stop and help. I walk directly to the door and knock authoritatively and wait.

Brick opens the door with a large, inviting smile. His eyes are bright and twinkle and the furrowed brow I had grown accustomed to is gone.

"Namaste!" he says softly and bows to me. I return the gesture as he leans in to hug me. "I am so happy to see you." And I can tell he is.

This is not the man I left 3 years ago. This is not the man that was filled with so much hate and so much turmoil that it was eating him, and me, alive. I had been squirreling things away, slowly packing those things that I wanted to take with me. I knew that I was leaving the bulk of my stuff, and I had accepted that. But I wasn't ready to leave the few things that couldn't be replaced. The Barbie my dad gave me for Christmas the year before he died, the photo album, my books marked up and written in from grad school, letters, those things I was moving slowly, so that I could pack up one night and leave.

When we moved, it was supposed to be a new start. He was supposed to escape the past and the reputation and the new landscape wasn't going to remind him of everything he hated. But when we moved, he had less than he had before. He didn't have any friends except me, he didn't have a job, he didn't have a direction. I worked, I made friends, and he resented me for it. Every day, we grew a little bit further apart.

When I would get home from work, he would be on the computer, with the headphones on and not even look at me. I would make dinner and he would let it sit there and not even look at me. I would go upstairs and get ready for bed and he would stay on the computer and not even look at me. He always ate after I'd gone to bed and he always came to bed after I was long since asleep. We weren't even roommates near the end, but it wasn't always like this.

Brick had sparkling green eyes that contrasted with his olive skin and black hair. He was the most striking man in my pottery class. He had a cool calmness about him, he was confident, but not arrogant. He was witty and funny, but always at his own expense. He was charming and sweet. We were the two in the class that couldn't seem to throw a bowl, or a vase. He excelled at the sculpting part, but anything on the wheel and we both were laughing at whose pot was more unbalanced. The relaxed banter in the classroom took us to coffee and then to the movies and finally to holding hands and that first kiss on my front porch.

He hadn't ever had a girlfriend before, he just dated and I hadn't ever just dated and only had boyfriends. We laughed and said we'd find ourselves in the middle. But we never did. We oscillated violently between it being the life I wanted us to lead and the life he wanted us to lead. We were friends with benefits to him, boyfriend and girlfriend to me. We were roommates to him, we were on the road to marriage to me. We were seeing where things went to him, we were waiting to have kids to me. But we never stopped laughing. We loved and fought with the same passion. We would yell and scream and throw things and laugh and joke all at the same time. We would wrestle and yell and insult each other and then make passionate love all night. We were full of passion, full of life, full of both love and hate.

Brick had left on a vision quest. He needed to find himself, he said. To find out who he was and where he wanted to be. He was gone 3 months and I was never really sure what happened, but he didn't like what he became out there and he lost the passion and was filled only with hate. He became suspicious and cruel. The laughing stopped and the quiet rage began. Like most women, I didn't leave because I remembered the good side. I could still see the bright-eyed young artist in there and I knew he would come out again. This was just a transition, something he needed to live through to make him stronger, to build his character. If I stayed, I could be the woman who reaped the benefits of being with a man like this; I just had to be patient. But his hate became stronger than my love and one day, as I was walking up the stairs and tripped, he yelled, "You're fucking pathetic! You can't even walk up the fucking stairs without tripping!"

All the love I had for him broke. I had always been clumsy, but I was kind and patient and loved with all my heart. When I realized that all he could see in me any more, all he could focus on, was the clumsy, I knew it was time to leave. I had to cut the cord and let him figure this path out on his own. It was in that second, on that stair that I knew what I needed to do. There was no more doubt, no more indecision, no more hope and optimism.

But now, I can see this is not the man that I ran away from, that I packed up my most precious possessions and left everything else and drove away as fast as I could, in the dead of night. A thief in the night, no goodbyes, no closure, just silent running. I was afraid then. Afraid of his hate. Afraid he would hit me. Afraid I would make him. Afraid of his sadness. Afraid of mine. Afraid that somewhere inside I could still see that perfect kernel of good somewhere inside him that would convince me to stay. Afraid that that kernel I saw wasn't really there, but the warm, gentle, man before me makes me exhale and know that I was right. That I was always right, but that we just weren't right together.

I return his hug and know that all of the emails that we had exchanged in the last few weeks were real. He had found peace and happiness. "I'm so glad to see you." I pause and those old feelings of apprehension are returning. Should I stop? What am I thinking? Should I alter my words? Should I speak as if there are eggshells and he is fragile?

"Happy?" he smiles broadly and completes my sentence. I nod yes and squeeze his hand which he has entwined in mine. "Come, sit. We have so much to talk about!" His house is warm and inviting and smells of sage and incense. He is wearing loose yoga pants and no shoes with a linen shirt. He is wearing a leather necklace with an Ohm pendant. His hair is wavy and gel-free, something I have never seen. Even when we were together, his hair was always perfectly groomed.

He leads me to a tan loveseat and sits down next to me. "I have been so eager to make amends with you," he says, his voice is earnest and open. And there is an ache in my heart. This is the man I loved, the one that I could always see inside of but the one that he didn't believe in and that didn't visit the surface much. This is the man I wanted to grow old with. This is the man that I wanted to have children with and write and draw and sing and dance and love with. This is the man that he couldn't be, with me. He saw the pain in my eyes and kissed my forehead gently. "It wasn't you, my love." He answers the conversation I was only having in my head. "I couldn't be this for anyone but myself. You had to leave. It was right. I had only hoped that I could come back." He paused and squeezed my hand slightly. "But I know now, that isn't to be. None of this," he gestured to himself like Vanna White, "would ever have happened if it hadn't been for you."

I smile doubtfully and think of the years that we spent together. The years of fighting, yelling, crying. The years of sleeping in the closet to avoid his rage. The years of asking my friends and family not to stop by, not to call, not to aggravate him. The years of waiting for him to see that he could be more. The years of seeing him fall deeper and deeper into self-loathing and panic and pain. The years of trying everything to

17

help him see and the years and years of him making me doubt myself and begin to believe all the things he said were true. The years and years it took for me to go from a secure, happy, loving person to an insecure, anxiety-ridden, cowering girl. And the years and years it took me to get it all back and the seconds it took him to bring it all back to the surface.

"All that time," he continued, "you gave me your energy. You gave me your goodness. You gave me your strength. Neither of us knew it, but you giving it to me, was taking it from you and it was being planted in me." He leaned closer and put his arm around me and the other on my knee. "It just needed time alone to grow."

"Maybe." I respond, quietly.

"Don't say it like that. It is true. You made it all happen. I would have died, during that time, if it weren't for you. And you sacrificed yourself. You gave me all of you and I gave you nothing in return. I borrowed your soul all that time. When you left, I thought I would die. But being alone and really looking at what I was without you, made me realize what you had given me and what I had lost. The only thing I could do was think about how amazing you were and how awful I had been. And I wanted to change. I wanted to become someone that you would be proud to know and to love. But the amazing thing, the miraculous thing. is that I didn't just want it to get you back, I wanted it because I wanted to be different.

I hated that person I had become. So hateful, so full of spite and malice. So controlling. I wanted to become something, more." He exhales and leans over and kisses me softly. "How is your life?"

"Good," I whisper.

"I'm glad you've found happiness. You deserve it." He leans over and kisses me again. I take a deep breath and try to exhale slowly. This is what I want, this is why I am here. I run my fingers through his hair and pull him closer. He pulls me over on top of him and kisses me gently, more gently than I ever remember being kissed.

"Things are different now." He speaks quietly, slowly. I nod "There is nothing but now. There is no past, no future, just two souls who have gravitated towards each other over and over and are here again." He slowly caresses my back and moves his hand up my skirt. "It was never wrong with us, it was just the wrong time. We are the same." Continuing to kiss me, he slowly moves us to the rug. "We have never been two, we have always been one. No matter what happened. I felt you." He slips inside of me and I exhale, "You can feel it. You can feel our energies intertwining. You can feel that moment that we are whole." He continues to talk, slowly, quietly. "I have often thought of this. Of the time you and I would be reunited. I never doubted it would happen. I never doubted you and I weren't finished." He is so gentle, so kind that it is easy to forget the hard years and give in, just be part of this moment. He is right, he isn't the future, he is only right now.

It is hard to remember the reason that I am here. To just stay here and get lost in this calm and bask in the adoration, but it is still there, a dark glint in his smile that reminds me of all the things that he is capable of. Of me getting off a plane in the middle of the night to a cold and desolate new state and riding a shuttle to the rental park all alone. Texting and calling and receiving no response. A land flat and barren with wispy trees and yellowing grass. I finally found the dirty and run-down hotel that I had booked near the airport and I was afraid to get out. The facade was cracking and breaking off and there was trash and holes all over the side of the building. When I entered the little enclave of the front desk, it had scratched and graffitied Plexiglas and it reeked of urine and stale smoke.

The toothless man behind the screen gave me a creepy grin and asked me what I needed. As I confirmed my reservation and clutched my purse to me, I wondered where else I could go in this foreign city at 1.00 am with me totally exhausted and my eyes and feet screaming for release. I took the sticky key from him and walked up the two small, dark, and flickering flights of stairs walking past room after room with noises ranging from screaming, smashing, blaring beats, and smashing escaping the doors. I found my room 213 and tried to open the door without touching the gooey splatter on the wall and door. I entered the small room and put the deadbolt on the lock and moved the small chair up under the handle. I sat on the dingy and holed bedspread and frantically dialled the phone again... NO answer. Text. All unread. I turned on the TV and looked out the window at my small white rental car that I had parked under a street light and what looked at the array of broken-down, tireless, and jacked-up trucks surrounding it. There were people standing all around drinking out of bottles and listening to the bass-driven music out of the trunks of their cars and the cigarettes that people were throwing all around the parking lot. I shivered and pulled the curtain shut and clipped it tight with my hair clips.

I called again. Again. Again. Noises from the hallway of men fighting and women screaming. Fighting and smashing and the door being punched. Punches and more screams. I grab my bag and the big blanket from the closet and retreat to the bathroom. The stale smell of smoke is burning my nose and the back of my throat and I dial again. And again. I go into the bathroom and lay the towels down in the bathtub and lie on top of them. Blanket on top. Lights out. Door shut and locked and stare at the phone. Text. Text. Text. **Where are you?**

Please answer me.

This hotel is the worst.

I think I might die.

People are fighting outside.

I'm scared.

Where are you?

Dawn finally arrives and I sneak, trying not to be noticed. Trying not to make a noise, and to escape without waking any of the night dwellers, I get into my little white economy car and drive away as fast as I can. Drive to? I am not sure where. Drive just to a place that I can feel safe. A place where I can go to the bathroom and wash my hands and feel clean. Just be somewhere I am not alone.

Ding. A text.

I pull over to a White Castle parking lot.

I thought we decided this was my weekend with her and you weren't going to interrupt?

And all I can do is cry because this weekend was all for him. To find a place to live, to find a job to find a place for us to move to so he can escape his demons and we can start something new, for him. And he doesn't care. It is all for him, but he doesn't care what I have sacrificed, what I am going through, because he cares about what he wants, what he is doing right now. And what he is doing right now is her. Not me.

"I want to do a healing on you," he says and awakes me from my memory and I can breathe for a second. I am lost between now, mission, and then, the agony of remembering how bad it really was. But, I have to push that from my mind, because whatever he did, isn't *who* he is and I am here for that. Deep breath in. Then he rolls over to grab his pants.

"Don't move." he says softly.

I suddenly feel cold and exposed and look around for something to cover myself up. He smiles and helps me to my feet and wraps me in a cream, chenille blanket, soft and warm against my skin. He lays me on the couch and bustles around the room lighting candles and incense and I hear the soft sounds of chimes mixed with light drums.

"Perfect!" he whispers. He kneels above me, "Just relax," he says, and his hands hover over my body and he begins to chant softly. I feel a warmth come over my whole body as he moves his hands up and down the length of my body without ever touching me. The chimes, his chanting, the low lighting and I feel drowsy. I feel like I am sitting next to a blazing fire with hot chocolate and s'mores. I am slowly drifting off to sleep when he stops and thumps my chest.

Suddenly, I am alert, awake and it hurts. I touch the spot where he hit and feel the pain continue to emanate. His chanting becomes more frenzied and he moves his hands more briskly up and down, but never touching me. I can feel the warmth of his touch beginning to invade my space, I can see a hazy blue light trying to mingle with my red light. I concentrate on the boundaries, I concentrate on not allowing his blue to take over and there is a little halo of lavender in between the red and blue. He smiles and thanks me for allowing him in my energy. "We are done here," he smiles, and offers me his hand. I sit up and get dressed slowly without fear of embarrassment. He wraps his arms around me and hugs me tightly, "I am so glad you visited." He says, "Please stop by any time." He smiles and opens the door for me.

As I walk away, I don't look back, I was there for less than two hours, but I have lost five years of weight and stress. I smile and drive down the hill slowly, not wanting to lose this calm, not yet.

Day 3
Jon

The drive across the desert is more grueling and takes much longer than I remember. I wipe the sweat from my forehead for what seems the hundredth time in the last half hour and scan the horizon; there is still nothing in sight but browning sagebrush and the endless line of asphalt. I have driven from Salt Lake to Reno countless times and I know every rest stop and gas station that has good bathrooms and snacks, the best cheap, but clean hotels and the best gas, but I have never noticed the turn-off described in his letter:

"Just before the beginning of the final hill before you enter Fernley, a dirt-turn off with a row of fruit trees struggling to find water. I will be under the shade of the largest one."

There isn't reliable cell service in this area and the maps didn't show it anyway. Without an exact address, I had no choice but to just trust myself, but I have already gone into Fernley, realized I went too far, got a drink and headed back out. I thought I saw the trees from the other side of the highway, but by the time I turned around, I had lost sight of it like a mirage and standing here in the brutal sun, I can't see anything, anywhere.

"Shit," I say and get back in the car. I pick up my iced Sweet Tea and feel the cool of the condensation on the side of the cup and rub it across my forehead, cheeks, and the back of my neck and finally take a long drink. I take a deep breath and exhale.

"This is it. If I hit fucking Fernley again, this is just not going to happen." I start my car and begin to drive well under the eighty miles an hour speed limit and stay in the right lane. There aren't a lot of other cars on the road, but the ones that are there pass me angrily for making them move lanes or adjust cruise control and snap them out of their zombie-like state. A few glare at me as they pass, a few wave, and one flipped me off.

I compulsively check the temperature outside, the car's temperature gauge, and the air-conditioning setting. It is too hot to drive without it completely, but I don't want to break down out here and I don't want my car to overheat. That has happened too many times in the past, hoping for kind Samaritans but fearing everyone was a sadistic rapist.

Someone would roll up and ask if I needed help, a ride and I would have to agree, because I did. I would eye their car suspiciously, the passengers. Were the wife and kid really his? Were they there under duress too? Were they drugged? Was that dog a man eater?

Were we headed to underground dog fights where they used kidnapped girls as currency? I'll bet my blond against your redhead that my dog pins yours in two minutes? Even when they dropped me off safe and sound, I looked behind me wondering if they were watching where my hotel was, who I was calling for help. If they had marked my car and would return later with their band of hostiles. I never felt safe until I was back in my car, doors locked, and busting down the highway at eighty miles an hour with my music blaring and the car's heater on high helping keeping the temperature down. In retrospect, it wasn't a good idea to be driving that twenty-year-old car across the desert every other weekend. But I had moved to Reno for graduate school and Jon still had a year at the U and his car was on blocks in his front yard and to a twenty-five-year-old girl, not seeing your boyfriend for longer than every two weeks was unimaginable and tempting fate with a horrible kidnapping and murder because your car continually overheated in the cruel heat was just a risk that had to be taken. Always checking that there were full gallons of water in the hatchback and unopened bottles of antifreeze, just in case. A sleeping bag, a tent, a few MREs and I was ready for whatever.

Now, however, I know that it is not worth it and check the temperature on my rented Saturn. It was hard to find a place that still had Saturns for rent, since the line had been killed years ago. But I needed the experience to be as authentic as possible, even though this car is several years newer than mine was, and the wrong shade of gray. It was rented hastily, at too high a price (due to the one-way nature of my trip) and I am still a bit nervous that the mechanics may not have been as diligent in the up-keep of this older model. Who knows how many times it could have been bought and sold before it made its way to "Save Rental"? I exhale and think, this is the final look when I notice a row of slightly larger, but no greener, shrubs just ahead. I slow and pull over to the shoulder, these are definitely not fruit trees, but they are also planted and are not natural growing sage bushes. I turn off and drive slowly, trying to disturb as little dust as possible when I see one tree, about two feet taller than any of the others and know that is where he is. I stop directly in front of the tree and turn the ignition off.

Getting out of my car quietly because I see him there, sitting with his back straight against the tree and his head tilted upward, his mouth slightly opened. He is still as magnificent as ever. He looks like a statue sitting there in linen pants and shirt. His hair is still jet black and thick with a slight curl, assuring me that it is real. His jaw is square and his expression stoic. His large hands are placed gently in the ohm position one on each of his folded knees.

Jon has always been a striking man. Partially because he is usually at least two feet taller than anyone else in the room, but also because of his classical Superman good looks and because of his presence. His calm, stoic nature made everyone want to talk to him, but afraid to at the same time. Giving him an air of mystery and allure that he never quite understood or believed when I explained it to him. As I tiptoe closer I notice that there isn't a wrinkle on his face, not even little crow's feet around the eyes. He looks exactly as he did thirteen years ago when I kissed his cheek and wished him happiness. I want to run my fingers down his face, to press my head against his chest and hear his heartbeat, to assure myself that he is alive and isn't just a shell of Jon. I sit down softly next to him and try and share the small patch of shade. We sit there silently for about 15 minutes until I feel him move slightly, then he sees the car and jumps up, and finally sees me. I am just getting to my feet when he lifts me up and swings me around in the dirt road, out of the shade and twirls me around.

"I knew you would come," he states. To be fair, I know he is exclaiming it, but no one else would. He says it in the same monotone he always speaks in. A tone that has never mastered the use of exclamation points. I smile genuinely and kiss him on the cheek and run my finger down his jaw line as I had wanted to.

"You look fantastic!" I say excitedly, "Like a twenty-year-old! Time has not marched along your face!" I say jokingly. He smiles and puts me gently down. I see a smallish backpack leaning against the tree. "So," I begin, "are you coming with me then?"

He looks back to his belongings and answers, "For a little while. I need to see my parents and visitors aren't allowed at the ranch." I nod, "But I am allowed out whenever I want," he adds paranoidly, and I nod again. "I thought maybe you could drop me back off on your way back?" I smile, thinking of the route I had planned it didn't bring me back through here, but I don't think the detour could be more than two hours at the most, so I agree.

"It's hot! Get in the car, let's go!" I head toward the door and notice he isn't behind me, he is bowing in the centre of the dirt road and I can hear him mumbling. I don't want to interrupt so I stand there, next to the car and feel the full impact of being stuck in the desert without escape for nearly fifteen minutes until he finishes with a sign of the cross and hops in the passenger side, sliding the chair all the way back instinctively.

I put the car in reverse and with a 10-point turn get the car righted and within moments we are on the highway headed towards Reno. Jon waited only minutes before he opened up his knapsack and pulled out a CD and popped it into the car. Seconds later I heard the low rumbling drums and high-pitched chimes growing in number and tempo. I roll my eyes and look over at Jon who is fully enthralled with moving the fade and tremble and bass on my unworthy car speakers. To find that perfect balance, he taps his foot and imitates the sounds with his low, booming voice. I know this is not a battle I will win, nor one that I even want to start, so I slide back deeper into my seat and bump up the cruise control.

"You really do look great!" I repeat, "I would say you were twenty-three? twenty-five tops! That is so crazy! But because you're tall, you always looked older."

He silently nodded at my assessment and as we have had this conversation before and I know he chalks up his well-aging facial features to the lack of expression that makes his demeanour a bit scary. I smile at him.

"You," he begins and hesitates, almost like he is looking for the right words. He may look the same, but he has definitely changed. "You look like an attractive woman of your age." He smiles lightly and I know he means it as a compliment.

"You always did know how to charm a woman!" I joke and poke at his ribs with an outstretched finger.

"I mean. You don't look younger. And that is not an insult. You should be happy that you don't look like an old crone. Being attractive at," he coughs fakely into his hand, "our age is about the biggest compliment you can be paid..."

"Except for you look fifteen years younger!" I reply, stifling a laugh and looking over at him familiarly, with the small twitch below his left eye and his perfectly shaped and mauve-colored lips. I take a deep breath. I worshipped Jon. Wait, it is most likely still present tense since I still won't speak my mind about his choice of music or not asking me if he could play it. I worship Jon. He has always been like a rock god to me, since the first day he walked in late to our very German, very proper, and very grumpy 1700th Century Literature Professor's class. When he was asked why he was late, Jon stood up really close to the professor so everyone could see not only the difference in height, but in stature, confidence, and sheer sex appeal. He looked down at the little man in tweed and said clearly, calmly:

"I just am." There was no other argument, no excuses, no apologies and Herr Berger fumbled with his words, he stuttered and muttered something out that no one, not even Jon at that close distance, could understand and motioned for him to have a seat. Instead of taking the closest seat at the front of the classroom as one who is late and has already had a confrontation with the professor might do, he turned around, scanned the room and headed for a chair in the very back, right next to the window. He took large, loud strides over to the desk, moved it back farther, took off his messenger bag, took off his jacket, bent over for several seconds digging things out of his bag and finally sat down and adjusted himself for the pitifully small desk. All this as everyone, including Herr Berger, looked on.

Finally, only once he was seated, had a pen, pencil and our first novel out on his desk, was the spell broken and our flustered professor launched back into his speech about not accepting late work and expected only the highest caliber in writing and thought and if you weren't willing to take on the task then to just transfer out right now, this was not the class for you. A screech in the back of the room interrupted him again and I turned my head, sure that the beautiful giant was about to just walk out, but he was just adjusting his legs and pushed the chair in front of him forward. The blond girl seated there blushed and tried not to look back. Our professor continued.

I found out later that Jon was six foot six and a half inches tall, black hair, blue eyes, and a genius. He wasn't just smart, or well spoken, but a deep critical thinker who could come up with the most astounding theories and ideas within seconds of reading some new text. I believe this is partially because of the extensive reading he had done his entire life. He was practically an encyclopedia of history, religion, war, romance, and all the classics of English, Russian, Greek, and French literature. But it was also because he had a near-perfect memory. He didn't have an identikit memory, and he often remembered actual conversations and interactions with people much differently than they had occurred, but when he had read or learned something of value to all of mankind, he remembered it. Usually, he could remember a book and a page or a documentary title and year.

He was a true intellectual unlike any I had ever met. He was Hollywood Handsome and he had a certain gravity about him that made everyone want to be around him. Yes, gravity in both ways, serious and also a pull, he was irresistible. Every girl in the class, and many of the men, wanted to get to know him, to be his study partner, to have him peer review their papers and get coffee after class, but he was unreachable. He always showed up late, a fact that Herr Berger never brought up again, and as soon as class was over he grabbed his sweater and his bag and was out the door in three large strides and no one could get his attention.

It was the third week of class. I had just given up everything I had ever known and moved up to Salt Lake to go to school and experience a whole new life. I was not feeling particularly shy, nor insecure and I promised myself that the next day, I would talk to him and that is exactly what I did. When he came to class, slightly early, I understood the significance and that it was truly meant to be. He sat down in his usual back seat by the window and I picked up my stuff and obviously moved right next to him. He glanced over, but made no hello or smile or encouraging gesture, but I pressed on.

"Hi." I began, he turned his head and nodded at me, still without a smile or even a cordial look in his eyes, which I could now see were clearly very blue.

"I really enjoy listening to you argue with Professor Berger," dropping the Herr that we all called him, not knowing if this blue eyed god was in on the class-wide, campus-wide, joke. He almost cracked a smile, then stopped, looked confused and said:

"Argue?" I nodded my head yes, thinking I was paying him a compliment, but he had shut down. He reached under his desk, grabbed his messenger bag and books and quickly strode out of the room. I looked around to see who was watching and I remember feeling embarrassed and confused and that I had obviously done something wrong, but I wasn't sure what it was. Just then, Herr Berger entered the classroom and looked around, noting the presence of a few students with a nod. I grabbed my grey backpack with the Smashing Pumpkins patches sewn on the front and walked out of the door, not as quickly as Jon, but as quickly as my legs could manage. I had to find him, I had to fix it; I had decided today was the day and damn if it was going to go down like this.

I first checked the chairs on the 2nd floor of the English building, I had seen him reading there before. When he wasn't there, I went downstairs and did the sweep again, checking twice just in case he was in the bathroom or something the first time around. I then checked the benches and tables directly outside of the building and then moved on to the Student Building. I checked the cafeteria first, then the coffee kiosk with couches and tables out front, and finally, the large formal dining hall that was only used on special occasions and had tables, couches, chairs and a piano set up for student use on regular days. Sitting at the middle table, with his head in his hands and staring at the cream table sat Jon.

I walked up, sat down right beside him and said, "I am sorry if I said something wrong..." I paused and he did not move. "I was just trying to get you to join our study group." Several minutes passed and he still didn't move, I looked in his ears to see if he had earphones in, if he had heard me, but nothing. Just as I was about to add another apology he looked up, stared right at me with a stone-cold face and asked, "Why would you want the freak that argues with the professor in your group?!" There was a slight inflection in his voice on 'argues' and the rest was flat, monotone.

"The freak?" I repeated confusedly. I could see the muscles in his forehead tense slightly and his lips pursed just a fraction and I knew it was now or never, if I didn't win him over right this second, I never would. "I don't think you are a freak..." I looked down at my hands not daring to look into his face for this, "I think you are amazing." I tried to keep my voice steady and with as little inflection as I could. "I wish that I could remember all of those dates and facts and lines from the book and have them ready when Herr Berger asks one of his rhetorical questions that he thinks no college student could possibly answer so he has to be so gracious and answer it for us!"

My voice and hands escalated, "I have had him for three grueling courses and this is the first time I have ever enjoyed it. No, looked forward to coming to class! I am always waiting anxiously when you are late, I know if you don't come to class, it will be a dud." He doesn't show emotion, but I can see a hint of curiosity in his eyes, so I go on. "That first day of class when you made him look stupid, I wanted to clap! I've wanted to clap every time you have opened your mouth since! I feel like one day, I just might!!" I am animated now and my hands and voice are bobbing up and down with each word, I can tell I am being a little loud so I take a deep breath. "Anyway," I say more calmly, "I meant it as a compliment..." I pause looking for the perfect word, but I just can't find it. "When I said 'argue', I meant it in a good way. Someone needs to argue with that German bag of air."

I stopped and studied his face, still no signs of winning or losing this persuasion, but he did look less tense than before and I decide to be quiet for a second and just let the moment be, let everyone walking by see us talking, let everyone be jealous of me. After several minutes of me biting my tongue not to fill the silence he asked, "Herr Berg-her?" I laughed, ice broken. I filled him in on the joke and we decided to go and eat Indian food to celebrate our new acquaintance. I would have liked to call it friendship, but he was insistent that we did not know enough about each other, nor our personal quirks, to call it a friendship and several seconds later added, yet.

Knowing Jon hates to relive the past, I smile at the memory to myself and glance over at him still singing and tapping along to his Tubule Monk music. He catches me looking and smiles. "What?" he asks sheepishly, almost as if he doesn't want to know.

"Nothing." I reply, "It is just really good to see you. After you joined up with that group, I wasn't sure if I was ever going to again."

He nodded his head in agreement, "The first few years were very stringent. They had to be. No calls, no letters, no modern conveniences. There is a building in the back for all the newbies to live; however, after a few years, when you are in the rhythm and you have found that quiet place in your soul where things just make sense, you are allowed to move into the main house. It takes some longer than others and a lot of guys think they are done when they hit that point and just leave, but the path isn't finished and you have just thrown all those years away if you leave. That is why I didn't. Now, I can come and go as I please, email, phone, still no visitors, but I can visit others. I very often go off into town just to sit and chat with people. No agenda, no fear. It is very comforting."

"Well, good." I wait to see if he is done and if I can find the courage to add, "I'm glad there is still some you in there." When I finally say it, minutes later, he laughs a genuine and deep belly laugh.

"I haven't been brainwashed or tortured or anything of the sort. I have just found the path out of the maze in my mind." He speaks gently and with inflection and warmth, so unlike the man of 12 years ago who spoke in curt monotone sentences, he is free with smiles and eyebrow movements, all new effects for him. I can't help but smile and turn his tubular music back up.

"Jon?" I begin several minutes later. He turns his head and looks at me square in the eye making me feel a slight shiver, raising an eyebrow as a reply, he waits for me to continue. "I'm worried about you." His expression doesn't change and he doesn't reply. "I mean, you are, hands down, the most intelligent, talented, gifted," I pause, not sure if the same point-blank conversations we used to have were still kosher now, but I plug on, "most beautiful man I have ever met. Hell, ever seen!" I smile and let out a little laugh at myself; he still does not reply.

"And you are living in a monastery? Cult house? Prison? Squandering it all." My voice escalated and I took a deep breath. Jon looks down at his huge hands and shakes his head very minutely. "I hope I'm not stepping over bounds here; I am just confused. You could be a writer, a musician, an artist, an actor, a professor, a public speaker... Actually, I can't think of anything you could be if you wanted and you aren't doing anything."

"A husband?" he asks genuinely.

"What?!"

"You heard me. I couldn't be a good husband. Even if I wanted…" His voice is serious and quiet.

"Yes, you could. We are almost 40, not 90! You can totally get married and have a career and do anything you want! What is it you want?" I ask without thinking about it.

"I want to be whole,' he answers with no further explanation. It was often this way with him, his tragic flaw was he thought that he had a tragic flaw. There was no amount of reassurance or worship that could convince him that he was fine the way he was. He looked at himself through outside eyes that didn't exist. He thought everyone was judging and condemning him.

I remember, once, we were sitting in the park and he was reading Tolstoy and reading sections to me that he found beautiful or profound. His blue eyes sparkled in the sun and his dark hair had strands of a lighter brown. I was memorized by his voice. The cadence of his reading, the rhythm of his explanations on how things haven't really changed in all the years and governments in between.

"I think you should go into Psychology," I interjected in between thoughts. Slowly, he closed his book, instead of just turning it over to hold his place and he rolled over with a smile — a genuine, stunning smile. "Why is that?" he asked with more inflection and humor than I was used to. Disarmed, I smiled sheepishly and nodded and whispered, "Never mind." Quietly. He sat up and scooted closer to me and lifted me up on his lap, "Not never mind. Why do you say that?" His eyes were eager and his movements were familiar and gentle. Always waiting for the moments when all the stoicism and misanthropy fell away and he revealed this other side that never seemed to come out, that when it finally did, I didn't know how to react. How to keep them, to keep this Jon around. He moved the long curls around my face behind my ear,

"That came from somewhere," he said gently, "tell me where." His face was leaning over mine, so close I could smell the sweetness of his tea on his breath, his eyes so piercing, his arms so strong and gently around my waist.

"It's just..." I began hesitantly. I was always nervous telling him what I thought, what I felt. I didn't know if he would disagree or fly off the handle and just go away. He was like that. He could burn bridges, cut off ties with no questions, no second thoughts. You are no longer worthy and just be gone. Over the years, I had seen friends he had for years just disappear in this way. His brother, his roommates, his church, his professors, his authors... it seemed nothing was immune to his will of iron when he made a decision and I didn't want to be one of those things, left along the roadside to never be picked up or thought of again.

Choosing my words carefully, I began apprehensively, "You are just so good with people."

He let go of my waist and pushed himself back on his hands, making a distance between us and exhaled loudly. I hated that sound. "Wait," I continued, "I know you think you aren't good with people," He leaned in a little, but barely perceptively, "You aren't good with groups, but one on one, you are amazing! Everyone wants to talk to you, wants to hear your opinion, wants to match wits with you." He smiled, slightly, shaking his head.

"I'm serious. Everyone in our classes wants to be in our study group. I am like the guards at Fort Knox!" He leaned in closer and laughed lightly.

"Maybe you should stop keeping all those hot co-eds away?" he offered.

"Ha! Fat chance, you wouldn't even know what to do with them if I did let them in..." I paused dramatically kissing him lightly on the forehead and hoping the moment hadn't been spoiled.

"And?" he asked.

"And, you are a scholar. You are a reader and a thinker and a studier. You watch people. You don't get down in the middle of the dirt, you sit up and watch it from afar. You are able to see things that the rest of us can't. You can take the pride and fear out of every situation and just lay it bare." He smirked with one side of his mouth and wrapped his arms back around my waist and I exhaled and relaxed a little.

"You are amazing at seeing what people need, what people should just let go of, what someone really is without all the show. You could really help people with this. If you were a psychologist or some sort of therapist, you could really help people get their lives back together and it would help you feel connected and worthwhile, like you were making a difference to the world. Like all the people you are always reading about. All these things you see in the books, they aren't any different than the problems people have now, you are always telling me that. The only difference is now we have technology to cover up our loneliness."

He was still smiling, slightly, but his manner had changed, he was no longer loose and merry, he was back to being stiff and distant. He stared past my head for several minutes and finally gently lifted me off his lap and rolled back over onto his stomach and picked up his book, but he didn't open it. Sitting there, I was afraid to speak, to breathe. I placed my hand gently on the back of his leg and he tilted his head towards me, but still looking away, "You really think I could do anything, don't you?" His tone was harsh, maybe even sarcastic. With tears welling in my eyes I moved my hand and whispered, "Yes."

***

"I don't like him," Ivey said bluntly. As my only remaining friend her opinion is all I have to go on. "Well," she continues, "it isn't so much him as I don't like you when you're with him." She sniffs and nods her head agreeing with herself.

"How can you not like him?" I exclaim in amazement, "He is absolutely perfect! Didn't you hear him talking about the forced conversions? About Vanity Fair and its contemporary significance? The thing about forced liberalism in a time where stringent conservatism is needed? I can't even begin to imagine what you expect if you can't see how absolutely amazing he is. He plays the guitar, sings, writes essays, poetry, he is very religious and is a true gentlemen in the fashion of the Mr. Willowby!"

"*Sense and Sensibility* is my least favorite Austen novel," she said in a huff, "and he may be all those things, but you are a pining little monkey. I don't think you said one thing, other than to agree with him the entire time we were out."

"When there is nothing to say, there is nothing to say." I responded.

"Do you remember when we used to go to ROCK Church?" I ask, he nods. "I hated that shit. I hated the self-righteous pastor, I hated the guitars, I hated the drums, I hated that it was held in a Cabaret Theatre on Sunday mornings." He interrupts me with a deep, amused chuckle.

"Well, J. What the hell were you doing there then?"

"You," I respond and the smile leaves his face. "At first, it was about finding God. After my dad died and I screwed over my whole life in SG, I was looking for something to make sense. I wanted that thing to be religion. I wanted to be swept away and believe so passionately that I couldn't live without it. I had tried philosophy, I had tried popularity, and I met you right at the beginning of my quest for God. I was in the middle of reading the bible and was attempting prayer. Then, when I saw you, I knew you were the nearest thing to God that I would ever be near. I shivered to the core whenever you touched me. I felt faint every single time you kissed me. I didn't need a higher power, because there was you. You were my higher power. You were my god."

"That is ridiculous," he replies in his monotone voice without looking at me.

"Ridiculous or not, it is the truth. I love you, I always have. But not like a man, like a deity. I gave up everything for you, I did anything you wanted, I lived to make you happy. I sacrificed everything for you... my opinion did not matter. We never had conversations, we had sermons where you preached and I listened intently and tried to sort out how to please you. I never felt guilty about having sex, I had dealt with that years before, but I feigned it for you. I wanted to have the feelings, the impulses you wanted. I burned with passion every day and would count down the minutes until you would hit the wall of weakness and take me into your arms again."

I take a deep breath and try and fight back the tears. "You think you are flawed. That you are running around in a maze in your head, but waiting for you to see how amazing you are, for you to do what you are capable of is what I have been watching, waiting for all these years. I believe in you. I worship you and I always have."

"Do you remember," he asks, "when we went to the Shakespeare Festival?" A broad smile spreads across my entire face. "Of course I do!" I respond.

I had never been to a play before, although I had been to many concerts and I thought it was similar and Jon had laughed at me when I said so. We had a 3-day package of shows, lectures, meet and greets, and festival dining experiences. I had paid for them, as I paid for everything as my version of tithing, but he had planned everything. He had scoured the plays and the reviews and actors and directors to select just the perfect line-up for us. We had traveled three hours south and as the temperature rose, so did the excitement.

We went to *The Tempest* the first night we arrived and as we sat in the audience, there was a buzz about the place, an excitement I couldn't quite explain until the actors hit the stage. We, Jon and I, were transformed into wall, we were privy to conversations and dialogue that no person could be. We could see the trouble mounting, we could hear the anguish in voices and the deceit in movements. We were not in a crowded theatre, but alone, voyeuristically watching others live out their lives and mistakes. The two hours passed with a blink of an eye and when the lights rose and the spell was broken, I felt weak and energized. Out of character for myself, I took Jon's hand in mine and kissed him passionately, right there in the theatre, under the stars, and I felt the power of having god on your side.

"That night," he said, "After *The Tempest*, was the night I loved you most. I loved our lunches, our talks, our readings, our chilling out while you cooked and I goofed around on the guitar or painted or whatever. But that night, you were so much more. There was a passion, a drive, a desire, in you and I always wanted to see it again. And the only time I did is when you told me that we weren't working and to please stop dropping by. I don't like to remember that time as much, so I think of that night instead."

"I wasn't ever really me with you." I try to explain, "I was your devotee and my point was to make you happy. I'm ashamed to admit it, but I still do it now. I hate this fucking music!" I turn off the radio with a dramatic flick of my hand, "But you like it, so I let you have your way. You have always had this power over me."

"I never asked you to sacrifice yourself."

"I know, but something inside of me just whispers things to me, my personal Holy Ghost named Jon Jr."

Jon shakes his head sadly, "I wish that hadn't been the case."

"Me too."

Suddenly, I see his face has aged, he looks older and sadder and I am afraid I have ruined everything. We hit the crest of the hill and overlook the sad and grey city of Reno and he puts his hand on my upper thigh and I exhale knowing that I am wrong.

I can hear the water splash as he moves around in the too small bathtub, a luxury I am sure they don't have at the "ranch." I take a deep breath and open up the door, he looks up and smiles. He looks like a little boy in a baby-sized tub, he is hunched down to have his torso in the water and his legs and arms spill over the sides. His face is half submerged in the water, making his butt sit on the front of the tub. Bubbles spill over the sides and make a sort of beard or mane around his face. He doesn't move when I walk in, nor does he speak. I move his arm into the tub carefully and sit on the edge of the tub, I pick up a neatly folded washcloth from the sink and dunk it in the water next to his chest. The water is cooler than I had imagined, I thought he would be sitting in a steam bath, I shiver at the surprise of the temperature and my nipples rise up, nearly peeping through the thin cotton dress I had slipped on as soon as we reached the hotel.

Slowly, as I wipe his sweaty face and trickle water down the top of his head, he sinks his head in deeper, which makes his body lift out of the water. His skin is creamy white and accented by small tufts of dark hair. I move to the floor and scoot down towards the faucet and dunk the washcloth again, this time, wiping his knees and down to his upper thigh. I watch him as he watches me and we both are silent. Suddenly, he sits up and wraps his huge arms around me and pulls me into the tub. He turns himself sideways so he is facing out with his long legs draping over the side of the tub, he places me, gently, in between his legs, directly in the water.

Wrapping both arms around me, he criss-crosses his arms and mine and both are held tightly to my ribs and he whispers quietly, "Are you sure?" I nod in agreement and he slowly begins to kiss the back of my neck, moving my dampening hair out of the way, he kisses up the side of my neck to my cheek and ultimately my ear. He slowly kisses my lobe and moves his hands slowly down, releasing mine from his grasp. I moan softly and move my hands down his thighs as I lift my wet dress upwards. He rubs his stubble on the side of my face and breathes heavily into my ear.

"Do you remember," he says, in a harsh whisper, "that night in Montana?" I nod with my whole body, lifting up slightly to get a better grip. He moves his hand in between my legs and slowly moves up my thigh. "We," he begins slowly in the same harsh voice, "were camping" a little higher, "and it was raining…" still higher, "there wasn't anything to do…" as he reaches the top of my thigh, he begins to go back down and I move my hand in response down his thigh, "except," he begins to move again and I copy his movements, "each other." He pauses and bites my ear gently, breathing out deeply onto the back of my neck. "So we did, again and again and again…" I nod again as he gently moves my hand away and lies back in the tub in the right direction. He moves my body slowly on top of his and kisses me, gently and then more ravenously. I pull up and smile and slowly pull the wet dress over my head and it pulls out the band holding my hair down and I can feel it expanding in the moist air. Smiling, he brushes it off my face with his wet hands. "I love it when it is wild and free."

"Me or my hair?" I ask softly.

"Both…" he replies sweetly and pulls me down to meet his lips again. He kisses me slowly, purposefully and unhurriedly. I smile and remember this, Jon is never in a hurry.

We were always late for everything… and it drove me crazy, but there was never anything I could do about it. No matter what time I told him we needed to leave, or I started to get him ready, it didn't matter, he would lie in bed reading his book, reassuring me that after just one more chapter he'd get up. Three later, he would. He would slowly walk around the house getting all his things in order, then finally get in the shower. If we were really late, the bath. He would take at least a half-hour soak, then there was hair and grooming and ironing and clothes changing. Nothing ever happened quickly and at the end, he looked pretty much the same as when he first started.

I began to write lists and make little stacks of his toiletries and outfits that looked good together, but it never really changed anything, he had to make all the discoveries and decisions himself. If I had all his toothbrush, hair brush, gel, razor and deodorant all in a pile on the bathroom sink, he would carry them, one at a time, to different parts of the house and have to find them all over again. I made schedules that were never kept, I turned off the hot water heater so he would only have a cold shower, he only stayed soaking longer. He walked slow, even with those long legs that took me three steps to each of his one, he walked slow and purposeful and I always had to turn around and see where he was. He selected each bite of food intentionally and took his time getting the exact proportions on his fork and chewed each bite thoroughly. He put his fork down and swallowed completely in between each bite.

I used to sit and watch him, in awe of how meticulous he was. Nothing was ever haphazard or accidental. He had thought out the proper way to do everything and took his time. It was clear that he had thought out every step of everything he did. I was always mesmerized with his thoughtfulness.

The first time we went to dinner, we went to The Star of India to enjoy a lunch buffet. He sat at the table first, ordering his drink and making sure all the silverware was clean and straight on the table. He then he got up and walked the whole of the buffet table slowly, looking at every item carefully. When he reached the end, he came back to the table and sat for several minutes, when I returned with a piled plate and asked him why he didn't get anything, he answered very seriously, "I have to think of the best combinations for each plate and how many times I should return so as to not get too much food for how hungry I am." He didn't smile or laugh at himself, he was very serious. I grew to love that methodical nature and even tried to imitate it at times… but I was never very good at it. The only thing I succeeded at was being patient with Jon and not making him feel rushed or like an inconvenience.

"Have I told you my theory on the man and two women?" I ask.

"I don't think so."

"Well, after years of living, dating, loving, hating, men I have realized that men need two women in their lives. One is the stable rock that loves them unconditionally and will always stand by them and will always speak the best of them, even when they are so filled with bitterness and hate that she knows all his weaknesses and insecurities. Even when they lash out at her and take everything she does for granted. Even when they aren't even a shadow of the man that she loves, she will still stand by him and she knows that and he knows that and he lashes out all the more. But nothing changes. Now, these two women don't have to be sexual partners, they really can just be any two women of importance in the man's life. Usually the first is a mother or a wife."

"And the second?"

"The second can also be anyone. A lover, a friend, a daughter, a sister, a niece, a daughter in law, any female that sees only the possibilities in him. Who doesn't see the bitterness of years in and out of insecurities and failures and meanness. A woman who sees him as he was when the first woman fell in love with him, funny, romantic, intelligent, witty, handsome, can move mountains. This woman serves the need of being adored. To put his best foot forward for, to be happy and loving and complimentary. Things he can't allow himself to be with the first woman any more. The pleasure of his company and the joy in her laughter will keep him adoring her. He wants to be, to everyone, including the first woman, what he is in the second's eyes." I paused and snuggled in a bit deeper, feeling the chill of the water on my legs.

"And?" he asks.

"And... we can't be everything to one person. Everyone needs more than one central person in their lives, but modern women can't seem to accept that. they want to be the embittered and then adored. You can't be both. Well, you can be both, just not to the same man. If you are the wife and will love them regardless of their failures and self-hate, then you need to find someone else to adore you. For most, that isn't hard. They have a dad, a son, a coworker. But some of us just play the embittered over and over again."

"I think you've been the adored more than you think." Jon says softly.

I smile down at him as I pull away and stand up, not letting go of his hand. "Let's go somewhere a bit dryer... and warmer." He gives me a sideways smile and let's go of my hand. "Give me 5 minutes." I leave the bathroom, shutting the door behind me, knowing that he went off schedule for our little foreplay session and he had to finish the bath and drying ritual.

I let myself air-dry in front of the air-conditioner and turn on the TV to a radio channel and turn the volume really low, barely audible. What no one ever believes is that Jon is magnetic and always has been. I am not only mesmerized but drawn to him, it has always been this way. This is not the first rendezvous we have had. Over the years, whenever one or the other of us was single, we would gravitate to one another. Even sometimes when we weren't. A few years after we broke up, he joined a band. Everyone was surprised and always second guessed his choice, but I knew it was perfect for him. I had gone and seen him perform in Denver on a layover from a conference and I was entranced, just as the hundreds of young girls were. He commanded the stage, not just with his menacing stature, but with his voice and with his energy. It seemed to spread out from his core chakra and expand to encompass the entire room. His voice was scratchy and loud and deafening and completely magical.

I couldn't understand a word he said, but I could feel the passion, I could feel the angst, I could feel the exposing of his bare self, the self without the rituals, the self without the fears, the self without the voices of a hundred opinions talking in his ear. Just him. When the show was over, there were gaggles of young co-eds clamoring to get to talk to him, but he didn't see any of them, he swept me up in a hug and squished me into his sweaty chest and kissed my cheek. It wasn't that I was his "one that got away" or that I was so beautiful that these college girls had nothing on me, it was that I knew and accepted him, just as he was. To him, that was the most important thing. I realized this too late in our relationship, far after we had ended the relation part and moved on to the friend part. All he wanted was to be important, to be real with one person. That was his world. He didn't want a gaggle of groupies, just one.

I hear the door opening and I turn around with tears welling in my eyes. "You didn't bring your guitar," I say quietly.

"I gave that up..." he answers neutrally. "When I joined the ranch, they wanted all worldly items. I gave them Old Betty and then, when I could have her back, I just looked at her, shiny and black and white and there was nothing there. Whatever I was trying to find in front of an audience was found alone in that house."

"But you loved it so much!" I interject, "How could you just stop?"

"It was just time. Maybe I will start up again, who's to say?" He smiles and lifts me up on to the bed, standing there I meet him eye to eye.

Nervously I say, "sorry about my hairs," I say as his blue eyes piercingly look at me, "I had straightened them this morning before I left but the heat, the car ride, and the bath all added a few hundred curls!" I pull both hands up the back of my head allowing my curls to tumble around my face uninhibited.

"I told you," he said simply, "I like your curly hair. You are the one who always felt it needed to be straight and in perfect place. I just liked it long. Girls should have long hair." He smiles, but I know he is being sincere. He is still very old fashioned and proper in so many ways. I lean over and kiss him, knowing that this is one of the things that it is OK for me to be modern about.

"Why;" I ask in between kisses, "Didn't you ever tell me that?"

"Didn't I?" he answers, "I thought it many times. When you would get out of the shower and your hair would be cascading in perfect ringlets down your shoulders and back. One of the most feminine things I've ever seen on a woman J." I kiss him again, harder and more intensely this time.

"I wish I had known you," I whisper as he kisses the side of my neck.

"You did."

"I wish I had realized it." He lays me down on the bed and as I am looking up at the ceiling, I feel him lay down next to me sideways. His hands move up and down my legs to my stomach, my breasts, my arms, my neck, my cheeks. I turn my face away as I feel the tears welling up again.

"What?" he asks kindly, quietly.

"I just hate that I lived in a box for so long. Things could have been so different," I gasp as he clutches my nipple between his lips. "Go on…" he whispers.

"I just think, if I hadn't thought of you as some sort of super human, things wouldn't have gone so wrong and you wouldn't be living at that ranch." He moves his lips to my stomach and over to the other side.

"I am not saying that we would have worked out…" I gasp again and take a deep breath. "It is just we could have taken better roads and if I had been different, we would have been different and you would have been…" I stop and he finishes for me, "Different?"

"Yes." I barely squeak out.

"I am happy J. That is all you need to worry about. Everything went exactly as it should have. I am right where I should be. I don't doubt that. Ever. And neither should you." He leans over and kisses me gently, powerfully. As he moved his mouth down my neck I added, "You are the man who taught me that I was enough. I just didn't know it until later."

"Really?" he asks as he slowly gets on top of me and pushes my legs open with his knees.

"Yes. Really." I reply, rubbing my hands up and down his chest and down his arms. As he draws closer I arch my back and add, "If I hadn't ever worshiped you," he inserts and we both pause and I gasp, "then I would never have realized that you worshipped me," I groan and move with him, "in your own way and that I deserved it."

"Yes, you do." he adds breathlessly.

"And…" I try and go on, "without that, I would never have realized how fan-fucking-tastic I really am!" He thrust himself harder and agreed, "Yes you are!" He begins to kiss me and the words are lost in the rhythm of our reunion. Slow and purposefully Jon and I took our time and enjoyed every minute of our time together.

"You," he begins, startling me from my concentration, "never needed to do anything to be good enough. I wanted to be someone you deserved. That is why I held back. Sometimes, I wish I hadn't…" he pauses to continue the rocking motion we had developed, "but usually, I am glad that I did. You do deserve better than me."

I sigh and moan at the same time, "Quite the Mr. Darcy complex you have there, sir." I pull his head closer to my face and kiss him, digging my nails into the back of his head and pulling his hair downward.

"Mr. Darcy is it?" he asks and flips us both over and he is now on the bottom and he is grabbing the back of my hair and pulling my curls passionately. I gasp and try and nod, but he has control of my hair. He lets go of my hair and slaps the side of my hip, I can feel the tingling and know that there is a red handprint there.

"I wish I could get a tattoo of that," I say and sink my teeth into his bare breast. His body lifts in surprise, pain, and pleasure. He groans and places a huge hand on my throat as he thrusts aggressively upwards and I claw at his legs. "Me too," he adds softly into my ear. Another furious thrust and he flips me back onto the bed with my head facing the headboard and he lifts my ass into the air.

"You have always had such a fabulous ass!" he adds as he spanks the other side. "Even if you have gained a little weight and started to sag here and there, your ass is still fan, what was it?" he stops and waits for my response.

"Fan-fucking-tastic!" I reply, emphatically.

"This," he said as he cupped a hip in each hand as he settled in behind me, "is why I always liked your hair unfettered. This is when I would see it, when you were like an animal." I could tell he was smiling, but we finally let the talking fall away and gave in to our baser natures.

***

I awoke a few hours later and looked around the room, it was still dark out, but I knew it was later than I thought and I needed to get on the road. I slowly walk into the bathroom and closeFhhes the door with the slightest click. I know I probably don't need to be this quiet, but it just seems like I should be.

Day 5
Zeke

Floating high above the town, Zeke and I are finally taking that hot air balloon ride... eighteen years later. I look at his thinning brown hair blowing in the breeze and the unmistakable excitement in his sparkling blue eyes as he points out the new arrivals to the town, since I left. He points out the houses that have been built where the old airport is and the large asphalt block way to the West where the new one is. His jaw has squared with age, but the hair on it is still sparse, little patches of stubble pushing through the tanned skin. His voice is as animated as his eyes as he reminisces about our old escapades, when we climbed to the top of that mountain for a picnic in the middle of the night, when we ran naked through the fountains on the University's entrance (it was just a Community College back then), when he and a few friends painted a huge star on a huge piece of plywood and carried it up to the huge D on the hill even though it was still so small you needed binoculars to see it, they had done it.

I smile and listen to all of his memories and then succumb to the joy in his voice.

I am not thinking about any of it right now, I am merely floating and I'm twenty again. All of the years and pains aren't here yet and I don't have to do anything, no pressures, no expectations, I can just sit here and float. I laugh at his memory of me getting on top of a rock and then being too afraid to come down and staying there for hours trying to build up the courage to climb down. He didn't leave me, not for a minute, he sat there beside me and talked about the life we could live up on top of this six by six-foot rock. He promised to build me a cardboard castle.

When I showed up this morning, at his work, I wasn't sure what was going to happen. I sat in the rented Jeep and waited. When I saw the Prius drive up, I knew it was him, I could feel it. I grabbed the tickets and stepped out just as he did. I paused and called out, "Zeke?" My voice was weak and shaky, but he turned around and I knew he had been expecting me.

He walked over in three long strides, not angry but also not gleeful, and stood directly in front of me, "Jules." He stood there and just looked at me for a long time, I wasn't sure what I should say, if I should get back in the car and drive away, if I should hug him and act cool, if I should burst into tears and apologies, but I am numb. He slowly leans down and hugs me gently, I hugged him back with much more fervor and he leans back attempting to gain his balance, we both laughed and I handed him the tickets. He looked down, turned them over, "July, 13th, these are for today?" he asked. I simply nodded and waited. "In an hour." Again, I nodded. "Come sit for a minute," he added, and we moved towards the small bench in the grassy area of the parking lot.

"Zee," I begin quietly, "I know this may seem a little, well, out of the blue. But we always promised we would go on a hot air balloon ride together and I haven't ever done it yet and…" I paused to see if he was still paying attention because he was looking down the road at the slow stream of cars beginning to stream in for work, but I could tell he was listening. "I am at a point that I really need to start doing some of these things. To stop just planning and plotting. But to get out and do and I just can't do this one without you."

Without looking at me, he moved his head in agreement and stood up and headed towards the building's entrance. I didn't know what to do, but I thought it best not to follow him, so I got back in the driver's side of the teal rental and pressed the address into my maps app. It would still take thirty minutes to get to the launch site, but there was still time. I continued to fiddle with my phone until I saw him coming back outside with a ball cap and a jacket on with two bottles of water and a few bags of peanuts and pretzels in his hands. He smiled and opened the door and hopped in, "This," he said motioning towards the inside of the car, "is nice!" He slammed the door and buckled up.

"Do you want to drive?" I asked.

"Nahh. I haven't been behind the wheel of something with this much power for quite a while, might be dangerous." He winked jokingly and I started the engine.

"Fine, then you navigate." I handed him my pink, silicone-covered phone and he smiled, "I'm not surprised," he said, as he proceeded to peel off the protective cover and tap on the screen. I revved the engine and reversed out of the space as quickly and roughly as possible and sped off out of the parking lot, waving and honking at all the cars entering.

It had all been so effortless. As if not a day had passed, as if so much pain, heartbreak, lies, betrayal, had not ever happened. As if the eighteen years that lay in between us had done nothing to change either one of us. We drove and talked about the blistering heat that has become more blistering every year, the tourists, the snowbirds, the drying up of the river, the new dinosaur bones that had been discovered, the new developments, the new off and on ramps on the freeway, the new fast food and shopping chains that had come into town. It was an easy, light conversation that took no effort and it wasn't hard for me not to bring anything up, to not try and apologize, to not try and make it all right, to just enjoy the moment. Where we were right then, and what we were about to do.

From the moment I saw the teal Jeep on the rental lot in space eight, right where they told me my car would be, I knew that this was all going my way. I had asked for a Jeep when I made my reservations, and they had tried to get me into a Cherokee, or at the very least a Liberty. When I insisted on a rag top, Scrambler or at least a Wrangler, I wasn't sure if the woman on the other end of the line was going to tell me it was tough luck, but she cleared her throat and said, "We have an off-road sister company, I will just go ahead and book you from here, but the reservation will be through them. You do realize that an older Jeep will get no more than 10 miles to the gallon?"

I agreed with her and the reservation was made, but I had no idea just how perfect this would be. It was a deep teal-ish turquoise and had a sun-faded black rag top with a reinforced roll bar going over the top of it. The tires and doors were still speckled with red dust and the door handle was at eye level. Patting the side plastic door window, I smiled and said, "I'm going to call you The Smurf Conspiracy" and I happily swung the door open and heaved myself up into the driver's seat, moving the seat as close to the steering wheel as I could and depressed the clutch and turned on the ignition. The bone-rattling noise was exhilarating and I smiled at there not being a radio. I wouldn't be able to hear it anyway, not with this beautiful noise.

Exiting out of the parking lot, I drove aimlessly around the city. It was just getting dark and the heat of the day wasn't yet rising and the air was suffocating, the Jeep didn't have air conditioning so I poured a bottle of water over my head and drove faster. There were so many memories, everywhere I looked, and so much new, so much changed. I have been back, I haven't just been gone all these years, but I never allowed myself the indulgence of remembering, of analyzing, and just taking it all in. Tonight, that was all I planned on doing, but I did have one stop I needed to make first.

Slowly, hoping it would still the noise of the engines just a little, I turned towards the top of town. Some cities don't have a top or a bottom. They are referred to in North, South, East, West and so is this one, by the newcomers, but those who know, who have breathed here, have lived here, know that there is a top and a bottom. A small incline makes the Smurf roar louder than I had hoped and the street lights begin to pop on as our approach. Everything is still and the flowers are all in their perfect place next to the perfect gray statues they stand next to. I park at the edge of the grass and start the long trek up the hill towards my dad, slowly. When I make it there, the small gray stone sticking out of the green grass seems smaller and colder than I remember. I brush off the top of it displacing leaves and small bugs that have made it their home. I sit facing the inscription and just stare.

I thought that I might talk, or cry, or have some sort of inspiration when I got here. But nothing. Just the cold gray and me. "Don't force anything. You don't have to feel or be anything that you aren't," I say aloud to myself and exhale. I pluck a few strands of grass and roll them around in my fingers, laying back, I feel the coolness of the ground reaching up into the heat of the night and know the cold is winning. I look up at the stars and know that I haven't seen stars like this in years. I move my shoulder blades back and forth and settle in, moving my knees upwards with my feet flat on the ground.

I can't really remember all of the specifics of his funeral, of his death, of the devastating boom that rippled throughout my entire being, my entire family, my entire universe. It is a fog. I remember the phone call, I remember picking a casket with my mom, I remember picking a song, and I remember seeing him lying in the casket, cold and empty. I can still feel that knot in the pit of my stomach that wouldn't let me think. I was standing there, in the blazing heat of late October and his hand was on my shoulder. He tried to hug me and to tell me that he would be there for me. I shrank away. There wasn't any place for me to feel comforted, there wasn't any way for me to let this pain disappear: that would be the ultimate disrespect. I shrugged him off and walked away. I still hadn't cried from my eyes; this was a vacancy so deep that only inner destruction of everything beautiful would be homage enough.

"Whenever you are ready, Jules, I'll drive you home." Zeke spoke softly, compassionately.

I look at him coolly and think about Todd. I had met him on my second day of winter semester. He was the epitome of a scholar; unlike anyone I had ever known personally. He read, and wrote, poetry. He listened and analyzed lyrics, he carried around a blank journal to jot down inspirations and sketch the little things he noticed. He was in my Shakespeare's Comedies class and he looked like Ethan Hawke in *Dead Poet's Society*. I was instantly in love. Not that I wanted to be with him, but I wanted to be him. I wanted to take on his airs, I wanted to transform and have people stop seeing the peppy, dumb girl and see a woman of depth and interest. I wanted to know everything he knew. I wanted to hear his opinions on every topic. He lived only a mile from my house in a little Airstream in and senior trailer park. That day, that Tuesday April the thirteenth, I knew that the insecure hesitant girl had to take a back seat.

After class, I walked up to Todd and began talking to him. I asked him his opinion on our professor, on Shakespeare, what his favorite band was. He was probably used to piles of admirers and thought I was just another worshipper, but he was wrong. I wanted to suck all of him in, so I could be a chameleon and copy him. I gave him my phone number and offered him a ride, anytime.

I spent every free minute with him from that day on. I would walk down to his trailer and we would climb up onto the roof and look at the night's sky and philosophize. I was hesitant at first to give him my opinion on anything, I just wanted to copy him. But as time wore on, and he exposed me to Rilke, Bjork, and the teachings of the Dalai Lama, I began to think past what he was showing me. I never disagreed with Todd, that was something you just did not do, but I questioned his reasons for thinking this or that and challenged him playing the devil's advocate. I felt myself expanding, my brain, my heart, my soul and I wanted more. We stopped worrying about class work and spent hours that turned into days eating from Taco Bell and discussing even the smallest of ideas. We were our own little think tank, our own clan of two, and then he met Ginger.

Ginger was in our Shakespeare's Tragedies class the second semester and she had that cool, confident air about her. She also carried around an empty journal and colored pens. She had long, bright copper hair and wore her jeans low and tight before it was cool. She was the first woman I ever met who smoked and made it look cool. She had funky jewelry from Guatemala and Peru. She had traveled the world and read Neruda and talked of Frida and Diego Rivera. Todd was drawn to their sameness and she loved him from the first hello. Then, there were three. We still spent all the time together, and talked in ever widening circles of thought and art. She was adversarial and wanted to debate every idea. We were still a clan, just a less loving one. Ginger was sure I loved Todd. I told her, again and again that I didn't, but she didn't believe me. I am not even sure if he believed me when I told him she was jealous of me and we needed to take a break from the three of us being together. He laughed and liked the notion of being in a love triangle battling for his affections. He didn't believe in expressing emotions through physical touch, so there was never solidifying of affection on either side, so the jealousy grew. The more she tried to get him to move towards her, the more I pulled away and the more he wanted me to stay.

"Let's go to the Indian Reservation today," Todd said as we were leaving class. Ginger and I looked at one another and waited for the other to answer, but I was the one with a reliable car, so I knew I had to be in or it was a no go. "I hear they have delicious flavored cigarettes that you," he bumped my arm, "may even like. And they are dirt cheap out there. We can sit out in the desert and just, BE!!!" he raised his hands above his head and spun around. Both of us smiled and said we needed to call in to our various jobs and roommates and previous obligations, but within a half hour, we were on our way.

The untold perk to the Indian Reservation in November is that they still had fireworks of all kinds for sale, in addition to cigarettes and cigars in every flavor, beef, turkey, buffalo jerky, and randomly herb and medicinal teas and baked goods. We all three charged up our credit cards as much as we dared and headed off towards the desolate mountains. We hunkered up with the trunk of my car open with a blanket as our shelter from the sun and smoked, drank, ate and shared all the deepest thoughts we had that day. It was one of the only times where the three of us were truly on the same blank page, writing in tandem with one another and honestly the best of friends.

Ginger and I discovered many more similarities to one another than just Todd and blank journals. We were both labeled and disregarded in high school, we both were told by close family members that we weren't smart enough to go or graduate from college. We both loved the Modernist writers and artists. We talked about Ray Mann and Mina Loy and Zelda and Scott Fitzgerald. We imagined what life would have been like, on the left bank of Paris right after the First World War. We drew parallels between the conservative, religious powers of the time and the same in our small town. We had both come to college on English scholarships and had both been "adopted" as prodigies by our Shakespeare professor. We were both red heads and when I expressed that I wished my red was more pronounced, she offered to help me to dye it when we got home. She was sure that just a little lifting would bring out my natural red undertones and I would be as natural a redhead as her, mine was just being stifled by the chestnut brown of mediocrity.

As the sun began to set, we began to make beds out of the towels, extra clothes and blankets in the trunk of my car. We all snuggled together under the blanket and sat too closely to the fire. We dozed off and were awoken, suddenly, by the bang of fireworks.

"This is OUR INDEPENDENCE DAY!" he yelled into the clear night sky. He was dancing around with a lighter in one hand and a firework in the other. He would light a wick and wait to set it down and run, he wanted to see how close he could be. "This is how you feel alive!" he exclaimed. Ginger and I smiled and were delighted in all of his glee. We watched as color after color exploded just in front of us. When the supply was empty, he lit three sparklers and handed us each one.

"Tonight," he began, "my ladies, we will make a skin oath to one another. That the things we have discussed, the ideas we have invented, the personages we have created, will be with us until we die. We will not comply! We will not assimilate! We will remain as we are no matter what comes." He pressed the burning sparkler onto his forearm and held it there until the fire was extinguished.

"I will not assimilate!" Ginger called out and we did the same.

Astonished, I sat and looked at each of them now tending to their burn wounds and stamped out my

sparkler with my foot and said, "I will not assimilate,"
I looked at both of them and paused, "to anyone."

It is not to say that that night was the end of our
group, because it wasn't as quick and painless as that.
We never spoke of the sparkler incident, but I knew
each of them thought of it. When we were lying atop
Todd's trailer and talking, palms up to the sky, their
scars gleamed in the moonlight and my empty arm was
turned over in shame. Ginger and Todd began
spending more and more time together, without me.
Todd's brother moved into town to go to school and he
moved out of the trailer and across town into an
apartment with him. For a short time, there were four
of us, but the four kept becoming pairs. As I would
show up and Todd and Ginger would be out so I would
just hang out with Rob.

One night, when I showed up and no one was
there, I let myself into their apartment and into Todd's
room. I lay on his bed, flipped through his books, and
listened to his music. I smelled the stale smoke and
muskiness of unwashed clothes and fell asleep. A
distant whispered declaration of love and devotion
awoke me. I could hear the hushed tones of two people
pledging their undying love for one another, no matter
what might come. I knew, before I had opened my
eyes, that it was Ginger and Todd and that it was over.

I wasn't broken hearted from a romantic slight, I
was broken hearted at the loss of a mentor, an idol. As
I gathered my stuff and prepared to leave, I saw his

sketchbook sitting on his computer desk and pushed it into my messenger bag. I walked out of his room and they were seated, entwined together on the couch. They were so engrossed in each other that they didn't notice me at first. I thought about just walking out, but stopped, the old me, the me that these two people helped me not to be any longer would do that. So I stopped.

"Hi guys." I said sheepishly. I was surprised that neither of them moved but just waved at me. "Just wondering if anything was up tonight?"

"We're just hanging in tonight," Todd answered, "Maybe Rob is free?" I nodded and walked over to them on the couch and kissed both Todd and Ginger on the top of the head.

"Thank you, Todd." I paused for a second and added, "I love you," whispered quietly to each of them and then I left the apartment.

It was late March and it had been nearly a year with Todd and later Ginger. I didn't have any friends outside of them any longer. I didn't know what classes to enroll in without them, I didn't know what to do with my time, but I knew that I couldn't be with them any longer. At the bottom of the steps, I sat and I cried. I cried with all the violence of a woman scorned, a woman betrayed, a woman abandoned, a woman afraid to be on her own. I sobbed so loudly that I saw lights turning on in the apartments next to me. I slowly got up and walked to the picnic table where we had sat and smoked and talked so many times and continued to cry in a more quiet, shameful way. I cried until I saw the night give way to morning and Rob just walking in from his night out. He looked at me, nodded his head respectfully and continued inside. Rob wasn't the type to interfere, if I wanted to talk, I would have called out for him, he knew that. Rob, I decided, I wouldn't have to let go of. I would just have to compartmentalize him into another facet that didn't include Ginger and Todd; after all, he was the only other friend I had. But I didn't feel lost or scared, I knew that I could meet, talk, and think with the best of them. I knew it was right, but that didn't take away the sting.

I ran into Ginger, years later in a coffee shop in Salt Lake. I saw her and knew instantly it was her. The years had not been kind, but her hair was still long and red and at a glance, she looked exactly how she had all those years before. She didn't recognize me, or didn't let on if she did. I was having a birthday party for my friends and as person after person came in and we greeted and hugged and talked about our lives and how much we meant to one another, I noticed her, sitting there alone becoming more and more sad. I should have, I admit, been the bigger person and gone up and said hello, invited her to sit with us joyous people. But I didn't. I watched her be sad and finally leave...

I had met Zeke just a few days later... still in the fog of not having a sense of who I was without my clan. He was always smiling, always joking, he had the most beautiful brown hair and dazzling blue eyes. He was thin and graceful. He was also relentless and complimentary. He knew my roommate and said he had wanted to talk to me for a long time, but I was always in a haze with those two. He listened to all of my stories, all of my ideas, all of my readings, all of my interpretations of lyrics. He sat next to me and encouraged me to talk, to be the lead in every conversation. Zeke thought that I was intelligent, that I was a philosopher. He wanted to hear my opinions, and mine alone. He would ask me question upon question on anything he could tell interested me. He took me to plays at the Shakespeare festival, he held my hand in the car, and kissed me tenderly at the door before saying goodbye. The giddiness, the energy, the tingling I felt in that second, I knew that Todd was wrong, and love should not be expressed outside of the physical.

"No." I answered coldly, "I already have a ride. Todd is waiting." And without looking at him, I walked away.

"That day," I start when there is a lull in his tour, "at my dad's funeral. I wasn't trying to hurt you. I, I just couldn't let myself feel anything good." I look over the edge of the basket and not at him. He looked at the pilot sheepishly, who was listening to a talk show on his phone and would occasionally chuckle to himself. He had clearly learned to not be present on these rides.

"Jules," he began quietly, and moved my head towards his, "let's not do this. Let's just enjoy this. Nothing else."

This is not what I wanted. I wanted to apologize, I wanted to explain. I wanted to give him all of the answers he had demanded all those years ago. The answers I couldn't give him then. But the steady gaze and slight pulse on the side of his jaw told me he was serious and so I relented regarding what I wanted and nodded. He smiled and wrapped an arm around my shoulder and turned me to the bright red mountain horizon and we both exhaled.

After Todd drove me home from my dad's funeral, I dug into the very back of my closet where I had kept his journal that I had stolen. I had never opened it, had never wanted to know what was inside of there, but now I needed to know. I opened the first page to read tawdry pop culture lyrics by the Spice Girls or someone, the next page had doodles of boobs and women's torsos, the next had Roses are Red Poems, the next limericks about our Grammar professor, the next and next and next were all filled with nothingness. There were no profound ideas, no sketches of beauty, no notions of love and life and death to get me through to the next step, nothing but the silly trifling's of a teenage boy. I felt the final piece of hope die.

I can't say that everything went back to normal after my dad's funeral, nor can I say everything fell to pieces. Neither happened. Life just went on, but out of me. I went to work, I went to school, I went out with Zeke. He did everything he could to mend the tear in my soul, but there was nothing he could do… but he wouldn't accept that. I graduated and I applied to go to university. I didn't tell him, I didn't say one word about the signed student loan papers, I didn't talk about the check being sent and cashed for my first semester at the dorm, I registered for classes and bought a meal plan. I filled out a change of address form with the Post Office. I changed my mailing address with all my bills. But I still didn't tell him. School was to start in two weeks and one night I finally said it.

"Zeke," I began calmly, "I am going to move to Salt Lake next week. I am going to go to the University of Utah." I then stood up and began to walk out of the room. He was stunned, he didn't speak, but stood and walked out of the room pushing by me. I stood there, wondering why there wasn't any feeling in me and fully realizing that I was completely dead inside.

As the balloon begins its decent, I see Zeke's facial expressions have changed. He wasn't smiling and his eyes were not ablaze with excitement. I lean my head into his chest. "Thank you," I whisper, barely loud enough to hear, but him squeezing my shoulder lets me know he has heard. These are the moments that I remember about us, when we were Jules and Zeke.

We were comfortable, we were easy, there wasn't any trying to impress or change, there wasn't any drama, well, hardly any drama. Before my dad died, we were as happy as two people could be. We went to work and I went to school and we spent every other second together. Each night was a new adventure, we were silly and uninhibited, we enjoyed every minute. Sometimes, we were curled up in a blanket fort talking about everything, but more often we were out creating new worlds. Dancing naked under the full moon, photo shoots in the high sunflower patches, wrapping ourselves in tin foil and grocery shopping, videotaping ourselves, karaoking our favorite pop song to mock, having art shows in my living room, making wakeboards out of garbage can lids, going line dancing, trying to make sushi out of canned tuna, impromptu Open Mic Nites in the park. We were the couple everyone wanted to hang out with, everyone wanted to be. We didn't fight, not even once did we have a raised voice.

We also made plans of what we would do, what our life would be like. We were going to go skydiving, hiking in the Grand Canyon, we were going to buy an RV and go to every National Park in the US, but for some reason, we pinky swore not to go in a hot air balloon with anyone else, ever. If we were going to go, we were doing it together and here we are, and it feels just like not a day has passed.

Zeke had worked at the college radio station, even though he wasn't attending classes, being of the right age range, having a love for music, and the procession of a silver tongue, he was still given a time slot. Listeners loved his infusion of all styles of older and contemporary music. We didn't have a very fashion-forward radio station at the time and so he would be the first place for a lot of music to be heard. Not just alternative, but country, swing, pop, classical, metal, rap, anything he found interesting. Once he found a new band, he was relentless about finding out who their inspirations were, where and whom they had sampled from and he would then make sets based on a new song and some of the older ones and influences. He smiled and told me once, "I don't want anyone to think Eminem was the first to use that beat, we gotta know our history. That includes music history."

He also used his show to talk with anyone who wanted to come on the show, or be a guest. DJ. Zeke was famous in his own way and when smaller concerts and art shows starting coming into town, sponsored by the college, he was the first person contacted. Publicists wanted to book their artists on his late night show, they wanted him to give a review of the album, to attend the show and promote it. We started going to every event in town. At first, it was really exciting, but then, it started to become work, but how could he refuse? Sure, it wasn't his job and he wasn't being paid for it, but he had a listenership that depended on him and the information he brought and how do you give up all the invites and comp'd dinners? Two twenty-two-year-olds couldn't.

"I know!" he exclaimed one day as we were trying to set the schedule for that weekend. Places we had to go, people we had to talk to, picking people up from the airport, being wined and dined, whatnot.

"Know what?" I asked confusedly.

"We can't stop going to things, clearly...." he said.

"Clearly." I agreed.

"And we can't pick one over the other because then we would be showing favoritism and I wouldn't know what to pick or not and I don't want that pressure." I nodded in agreement, "So, we just need to make everything fun! No matter what it is, we will do it our way! We don't have to act or be anyone! More exactly, we can BE anyone we want!!" He stood up and arced his arms over his head dramatically. I just stared at him and he chuckled at me.

"From now on, we are going to bring everyone with us! Spam, Pin, Payme, Pawn, Flash... anyone we want! And we are going to have a theme. We aren't just gonna show up in our boring old clothes. We will go as '70's disco-downers, or big '80's with jelly bracelets and shoes, even me." He winked and moved his eyebrows up and down jokingly. "Or we will be super heroes, or zombies, or baseball players, or German tourists, or avant gaurde artists!!" His voice continued to escalate with excitement. "We will make a fish bowl of the wildest ideas we can think of, things that put grocery shopping in tin foil to shame, and then we'll just pick one for each evening and go for it. FULL FORCE!" He hammered down his hand in the air and smiled a brilliant, convincing smile. "We will not worry about being late or leaving early. If we aren't feeling it, hey, we tried. If we love it, then we'll party it up baby!" He pulled me up from the couch and began swinging me around the room like we were ballroom dancing. "We can be svelte swing dancers!" and he dipped me. Laughing, I threw my leg in the air with a pointed toe. He kissed me and said, "If we have to do this, lets fucking enjoy it!" I smiled but added, "Language, please." He released the dip and kissed me again.

That was the beginning of the craziest summer of our life. We did everything he planned, we requested a huge number of tickets for concerts, dinners, cocktail parties, and we brought all our friends and wore whatever crazy costume we could invent with the things we had in our houses from the strip of paper from the fishbowl. We took bi-weekly trips to the cheap second-hand clothing store looking for anything totally funky and workable and not more than $1.00. We also would go to yard sales in the older neighborhoods, if we were up that early. We had a huge plastic tub shaped like a chest, curved lid and all, and it was full of last-minute items for people to grab if they had missed the theme or were without supplies.

When we had exhausted the ideas in the bowl, we began to put in movie titles and we would go in as characters, then we began going as musical artists, and then zombie versions of both. Our crowd slowly began to expand and everyone wanted to know what we were coming as and wanted to be included, when the college was having its Spring Formal, the committee asked Zeke what the theme should be he was still not in school. We decided on Mobster Chic and we had a party of over 500 people dressed just as we had told them to, and we were the King and Queen of the dance… if they had crowned them. I wore a black lace dress with a nude colored full slip so it looked like just lace over skin, he wore a black three-breasted suit with double holsters and a fedora.

Looking at him, he was still that young guy and I could almost see the fedora on his head. As we awkwardly get out of the balloon and thank our pilot, Zeke stops for a few minutes to ask him a few particulars about the steering and landing of the balloon and to ask how long he had been flying and if he liked it, always the perfect gentleman. I smile and slide in the passenger side and slip the keys in the ignition. As he walks towards me he smiles and slides into the driver's seat. "Well, all right!" he exclaims and revs up the engine. I wanted to let him drive, knowing how much he loved Jeeps, his Jeep, but I also didn't want to have to decide where we were going next. "Doesn't this thing remind you of La Jupe?" he says excitedly. I nod.

"I named her 'The Smurf Conspiracy'..." he replies with a hearty laugh and adds, "God, I loved that thing. She broke down on me all the time, didn't have air conditioning, and was a bitch to get in and out of, but I had some good times in that thing." He speaks honestly and without a hint of anger or sorrow. "I'm sorry about that too," I add.

Zeke slams on the brakes and sends us both lurching forward. "No more," he says calmly. "I admit, I was a bit surprised to see you..."He takes in a deep breath — "It has been a really long time. But it has been nice, this has been nice. I have never felt like I could go up in a hot air balloon either, so I am glad you showed up. But for shit's sake, you need to relax and stop apologizing. If I needed and apology, it was twenty years ago, not now! Please, just stop." Tears have welled up in my eyes but I am determined that this will not be on my conditions, but his. No tears, no sorries, no making up for past mistakes, just now. I smile as I think this is who he has always has been, worrying about now. Enjoying life as it is, in this moment, at this time. He had often reminded me of the Buddhist teaching of being present. Something I spent many nights trying to comprehend after he was gone. How to put regret behind me and just be in the now, to forget what came before and the names and the jokes and the chastisement and just be.

But I have so many things that I regret and want to apologize for, not for him, but for me. To let him know that I understand now, that simple isn't stupid and easy isn't not meant to be. I was so sure that you had to over-think, over-process, over-work every issue, every item that came about or you weren't intelligent, you weren't worthwhile.

I knew he loved his Jeep, it was a deep turquoise, not the color of The Smurf, but close. It was made for off-roading and mudding. He spent every weekend washing and polishing that Jeep. We named it La Jupe, the skirt in French, because he treated it like a fine linen that needed careful attention. It was noisy and hot and a gas guzzler, but he never complained about it, not even once. One day, when I had spent too much time thinking and thinking about my future and what my ideal husband would have to have or not have, I realized I could never marry anyone who had a Jeep and a noisy, unreliable one at that.

At lunch the next day, I told him as much. I had thought that it was my break-up speech, not because I had decided to break up, but because I was always testing him, testing how much he trusted my mind, my logic. Would he listen to my voice of reason? And if not, clearly that meant that he didn't think I was smart enough to be trusted and no one can be expected to stay with anyone who doesn't believe you are smart enough. These circles of crazy thought were very often the webs of my mind that I would get tangled in. I could see the final outcome, or thought I could, but once my mind had decided it was the only possible proof of trust and intellect, I couldn't step back. As he listened to my case against La Jupe, he asked, "Don't you like her?" to which I responded, "Yes. I like her fine. She is fun and very beautiful, but she isn't logical and it doesn't seem very smart to cling to a car that is so…" I paused and he finished, "Illogical?" I nodded.

That afternoon, he detailed her perfectly one last time and put a 'For Sale' sign on her in the parking lot of the local grocery store. By six o'clock he had five offers and La Jupe was not his anymore. He never, even now, brought up the fact that I am the one who asked him to do it and that he regretted it.

We drive in a comfortable silence until the edge of town when I begin to wonder, what now? As he turns down Elm Avenue, I know he is returning to the point of origin, I exhale because at least I know what is coming next. I want to turn on the radio, to play the song that is queued ready for us to listen, but the roar of the engine and the comfort seem to ask not to be broken. I begin to sing inside my head, to try and fulfill this moment as I have imagined so many times.

It wasn't "our song" necessarily, I am not too sure we had a song, but we both loved *The Counting Crows* and Adam Duritz was an inspiration to Zeke. He had started playing the guitar after their first album and he also credited Adam's free spirit as to why we became alternative people all summer. The night I had told him I was leaving, I heard his sign-off on the radio and he asked me to call him, to let him go with me, to think of us and all those "Perfect Blue Buildings" in Salt Lake City and he played the song. I wanted to call, I wanted to try and explain, but I knew it would just make everything worse, so I let it be and I didn't do anything but sit and cry. To this day, every time I listen to the Crows, I think of Zeke and when they were playing in town a few weeks ago, I knew I had to go and when they played a minor hit from nearly twenty years ago, I could feel the significance, I began recording after the first verse when I got my tears and wits about me. I had the song loaded, to tell him how I stood there and expected him to be behind me when I turned around, but I just couldn't, I had to let it be. I had to respect what he asked for, what he needed.

Instead I begin, "Do you remember, by chance," I begin as peppy, but not shakily, as I can, "that song that you and Spam sung for me that day in LA?" A huge smile spreads across his face and he chuckles. (We nicknamed almost everyone back then, he was Goat, I was Jules (not very creative, but finding a nickname for me has always proven difficult. My roommate was Pin, and his best friend was Spam, named for his unnatural craving for the gelatinous meat product).

"Ya know? Not really." He shifts his weight in the seat and coughs lightly into his hand, "I think I could maybe pluck out a bar or two if I had a guitar, but the words? I'm not sure?" He continues to smile and tap his fingers in rhythm on the steering wheel.

In the early fall after Zeke and Ginger left my life, I decided that I was going to go to Europe. After talking to Ginger, I was adamant that I was going to be well traveled, I was going to have stories of places I'd seen and been and I was not going to waste any time. I started a savings account and told everyone not to buy me any presents for Christmas or my Birthday, I just wanted to have money for Europe. I had then met Zeke and we had been dating for a few months before I finally told him of my plans and immediately, he wanted to come. He had made his case for getting off work, that he could save the money easily (since he wasn't in school), that together we could experience and see so much, but I said no.

I had decided that this was something I was going to, come hell or high water and in that vision, I was alone. I think most people would be grateful to have a traveling companion, but I thought it would tarnish the experience, close me off from doing and meeting the people I was destined to meet. I have since learned that I have a problem with being too stubborn when I think I am right, and this was one of those times. I was insistent that he not go but we agreed he could pick me up at LAX on my return.

I had a miserable and lonely three weeks in Europe. With pictures and thoughts to fill a book three times over, but no one to share it with, no one to daringly go out into the night with, no one to remember with me the horrible meat from that street vendor in Rome, or the delicious pastry in Paris. I did not want him to know that he had been right, that I should have let him come and that I had been regretting my stubbornness since the second day in Amsterdam. When I got off the plane and was walking towards the baggage terminal I heard my name, STAR something, something, something, STARRRRR!! And there was strumming and drums beating.

I looked around and Zeke and Spam were sitting on the ground directly outside of the cordoned-off area singing a song. Spam had on his silly Bob Marley hat with fake dreads and a tie-dyed T-shirt, SPAM playing dedicatedly to the rhythm of their song. Zeke was wearing a hat with little antlers on it and wearing all brown, playing his guitar with silver STARS stuck all over it. They both had huge smiles on their faces and a huge pile of sunflowers lay at their feet. I stopped cold and tried to swallow the lump in my throat, tried to fight back the tears. The weeks of regret and loneliness, the sorrow, but as they hit the second chorus I broke down and dropped my luggage and ran and hugged and kissed Zeke through the barrier. A nice man picked up my backpack and handed it to

Spam who was still drumming even though Zeke had long since stopped singing or playing.

I told him everything, how he was right, I should have let him go and it was awful and I was miserable but I had taken a lot of pictures, of everything I could think of, to remember to tell him every detail. I swore we weren't going to sleep for three days while I relived the entire trip so it was just like he was there. He kissed me and never said I told you so or you finally admitted you were wrong about something. I am not sure if he even thought of them, but I did. He now had the ultimate upper hand; I had admitted fault and there was no taking that back…ever.

"Well, My Star…" he began with a genuine warmth in his eyes and voice, "it has been great seeing you. I am really glad you did this. A little notice might have been a good thing," he paused, "but good for you, living in the moment." He turned and smiled at me as he turned off the Jeep that shuddered and bounced to sleep. I smiled and shrugged, not sure how to proceed.

"I am staying at the Fairmont Inn, Room 213, please come and see me tonight. I would like to talk to you alone." I hurriedly opened the door and got out of the Jeep, slamming the flimsy plastic door closed the best I could and walked around the back of the Jeep. He met me in the middle and handed me the keys, careful not to meet my eye. "Please," was all I could add. He leaned down and hugged me, my arms trapped at my side making it an awkward one-way hug, I tried to hug him with my chin, with my mind, to let him know I had wanted to hug him all day.

"I don't think that is a good idea." he replied.

"Maybe not, but please come anyway?" I asked. He looks down at his shoes and then over his shoulder at the entrance to his building.

"When?" he asks quietly.

"Whenever. I will be there all night. I won't leave my room, even for ice. Come when you can." I step up onto my tippy toes and kiss his cheek and walk as quickly as I can to the door, open it and climb in, I don't want to give him time to say anything else. He turns and waves and walks quickly into the building. I start the car and drive out of the driveway. In my mirror I can still see his form walking down the long corridor of the big glass building. He has to come! I yell at myself, HE HAS TO COMEEEE!

"Two cheeseburger meal, plain, with fries and a coke. Regular size." Ordering at the McDonalds I have been at a million times, I feel a cold chill run down my spine as I recite Zeke's order, not even thinking about what I would like or looking at the menu. "Shit." I mutter as I continue on to Window Two.

Entering the hotel room with a bag and cup, I sit on the floor and try and think about what next. Will he come? Will he not? Is there anything else I should have done? Could have done? I eat my fries slowly and think about the candles that had come in so handy, to set the mood in the other two cities, but there is something that feels unauthentic, unnatural in this case. There can be no long baths, no lavender-scented candles, no champagne or strawberries. The room has to stay as it is, but I do not. Hurrying through the last bit of my dinner I head directly into the bathroom.

Bath, shave, pluck, scrub, shower. Every wayward hair has to go and I can't look like I have spent the evening grooming, but that this is just how I am, all the time, now. I pull my hair up in a tight low pony tail and then wrap it around and secure it with a clip, the soft reddish ringlets drop over the clip giving me the illusion of short hair. I never had hair below my chin when I was with Zeke and he often told me how important that was to him, that girls were too caught up in their hair as a security blanket and hiding their faces behind curtains of hair.

I will admit that I have done that in recent years and even thought of cutting it off yesterday, but I wasn't quite ready to be without my security blanket again. I dab a little bit of concealer on and below my nose and my chin just to reduce the red, but not enough to look like I have any make up on. I put on a mauve lip stain and brush a non-glittery bronzer in the shape of a T from my forehead to the tip of my nose. We hadn't discussed a time, there could be a knock at any time, or none at all. I hurry, just in case. I select a pink and white striped sear sucker night gown with spaghetti straps. It is a little sexy, a little school girl, and still a little modest. All necessary facets in this case, I think. I hope.

I sit back down on the floor and stuff the McDonald's bag and cup into the trash and just stare at the door. I don't know what else to do. I could read, watch TV, pace, pack and repack, but I just don't have the energy for any of it. If tonight doesn't work out, it has all been for nothing and I will go home a failure. I take a deep breath and shake my head, "I can't think that!" I say out loud. He was so kind, so warm, so gentle today. He will come, everything is going to be all right.

"Has he ever refused you?" I ask myself and answer with a pause. "Yes. Once."

"Well, once is a pretty good record, bitch." I reply.

Maybe, but it was a pretty big once. When I say I haven't seen Zeke in eighteen years, that is a bit of an exaggeration, I don't count the last time, because I can't bear to think about it. It was two years after I broke his heart and moved to Salt Lake and was dating Jon. He transferred jobs, he bought a 4-wheel-drive truck for better use in the snow than off roading, and he called me. I didn't answer and he left me a message that he had moved up and he would love to get together, to just talk, to heal old wounds and have closure he had said. I wrote down his number in Sharpie on the avocado fridge, but I didn't call him. When Jon asked whose number that was, I lied and said an old girlfriend from St. George who I might meet for coffee. But I still didn't call. Jon asked again and again if I had met up with my friend and my answer was always no.

Then, I got the call that my aunt had been in an accident and her two-year-old daughter was an orphan. Both of her parents had died instantly and there wasn't anyone to take her. My grandma was too old, my mother too damaged after the death of my father, my sister too young; they wanted me to adopt her. How could I adopt her? I studied Jon over dinner and knew that he was twenty years away from being ready for a family, thirty from actually taking any steps towards one. There wasn't anything I could do to change that timeline. I hid in my closet for three days. I called in sick from work, didn't answer the phone and didn't even talk to Jon. I didn't go to the funeral. I didn't respond to any of my grandmother's pleas to call her or my mom. I was numb, again. Finally, I escaped myself. I showered, ate a small sandwich and a huge cup of coffee and dialed the number on the fridge.

We had agreed to meet at the park by where he lived at seven p.m. I didn't realize it would be dark already and I was poorly dressed for the night air. We greeted each other timidly and Zeke could tell I was cold and walked me to my car, opened the driver's door and motioned for me to enter and then closed the door carefully and slid into the passenger seat. From there he grabbed the keys from my shaking hands and started the car and turned the volume on the radio to low, but not off. I could hear the song faintly and concentrated on the lyrics as I tried to figure out what to say. He asked about school and told me about his transfer and his roommates and his house and where he liked to hang out now. He talked about the old gang and who was living where and who had broken up with whom and who had married whom. I partially listened, I partially concentrated on the song, and I partially thought of my own words. Finally, mid-sentence I interjected, "Zeke, will you marry me?"

I exhaled. There it was out. Now there was nothing more I could do. It was all up to him.

He stopped what he was saying and asked me, "What?" and I repeated myself. He got out of the car and walked around the park one, two, three times and then I could see he was coming back to the car.

"What the hell, Jules?" he said before he was even seated. I didn't respond but looked at the ticking digits on the clock.

"We haven't seen each other in over two years. You moved up here without even really talking to me about it and then never called, never wrote. No one heard from you! No one knew if you were dead, on drugs, kidnapped! Do you have any idea how worried we all were? Spam, Pin and I drove up here a shit-load of times, just seeing if we could find you! We never did. Finally, I met someone who knew your roommate at the dorms. Your fucking ROOMMATE! That is how we got information about you. You didn't just dump me, but all of the people that cared about you. Your mom didn't have any way to contact you. She just said you always called but there wasn't a schedule or a plan because you were afraid someone would find you. What the fuck would be so bad if we FOUND you?! What the hell was I, Spam, Pin, Payme, Pawn anyone going to do to you?" His voice was growing harsher and harsher and the tears began to stream down my face. I didn't answer. I continued to concentrate on the clock and the lyrics. Willing myself not to be here right now.

"Honestly…" he began much softer, gentler, "If I am really honest with myself. There is nothing I want more in this world than to say yes. To take off to Vegas and get married right fucking now. To just ignore everything that has happened." He paused and I dared look at him for just a second, but his face was not joyful or that of a man who was just about to go off on a hair-brained adventure, it was solemn and I didn't want him to go on. I didn't want to hear any more. His answer was no and that was all that mattered.

"OK." I whispered. "You can go. I really have to get home. My aunt died and I should call my grandma." He looked at me dumbfounded.

"What? When? Who?" he asked with genuine concern, the stress of his previous words vanished. He grabbed my hand and held it to his chest. "No one should suffer so much loss," he croaked out. I half smiled and told him of my aunt's accident. I did not tell him about my cousin or my grandma's request. If he was going to marry me, I wanted it to be because he still loved me in spite of everything and not because there was an orphan that needed saving. I knew Zeke and I knew he would forget everything and marry me right now for her because it was the right thing to do. His stepdad had married his mom when he was little and saved him from being an orphan at fourteen when she died. I knew that I could just utter those words and everything would be different. My life would be different. It was another moment of two clear paths, but that one had a cloud of regret that I could actually see and so I didn't walk down it.

After a few more minutes he added, "My Star," his voice was soft, gentle, and calm, "I am not saying no. I can never say no to you." He smiled and kissed my hand which he still held. "But I can't right now. We need to start again. We need to see if we still fit. We need to rebuild trust. You have a lot of people to apologize to and it is important to me that you do that. For them, but also for yourself. I can't say yes now, but I'm willing to leave it open." He looked at me so full of hope and the twinkle of love in his eye and I knew Jon would be waiting for me at the house by now. I had told him to meet me, not sure if I was going to tell him I was getting married or that we needed to go visit my family.

"I'm sorry, Zeke." I croak, "It is a yes or no question. I NEED to know if you will marry me right now. If you love me, if we can work it out. It must be now. Or it is a no and I am leaving again."

There was a long heavy pause and he answered, "You know this is not what I want. But you had better leave."

I started the car before he was out and was in reverse and leaving the parking lot with the passenger door still open. I was crying so hard that I couldn't see the lines on the road and I ran a red light. I was only a few blocks away from my house and I just drove there by memory. As I drove up, I saw CR4 in the driveway and I fell into his arms and sobbed until my head hurt and I was too exhausted to cry any more. I had to tell my grandma that there wasn't any way I could adopt a baby and she should give her to the state as my mom suggested.

Sitting here now, on this hotel floor, remembering Zeke's face, I should feel like this is a book long since closed. A tomb buried deep, deep underground, but I don't. I never have been able to admit that Zeke and I are completely over. I look at the clock and it is 11.29 and I wonder, for the first time in sixteen years if I am wrong. I lean my head to my knees and try not to cry. I can feel the deep ache, the strong, body-breaking sob in the back of my throat and I struggle to keep it in.

"Star?" I hear Zeke's voice just outside the door with a soft tap of his fingertips on the door and I stand up, rustle my hair, and open the door with a mock sleepy smile.

"Hey," I say quietly as I open the door wider for him to step in, and as he does he quickly replies, "I brought you something."

"What?" I ask, honestly confused and my eyes dart to the box in his hands, not fast food or anything I could have left with him today.

"This!" he says and hands the box to me like a three-year-old giving a gift. His eyes gleam with pride. I slowly open the lid and dig through the newspaper wrapping and my hands hit on a smooth object, I pull it out slowly and see the swirly, curlicue designs of paint on wood, it is dark blue, light blue and white. Once I get it completely unwrapped I see it is a set of Babushka nesting dolls. I twist the largest one open to reveal the next one, then the next, then I sit on the bed so I can continue to untwist all eight of them.

"Oh Zeke!" I squeal excitedly, "I have ALWAYS wanted one of these!" He smiles and adds, "I know, you once told me. When I was in Russia on vacation, I saw this and I just couldn't help but buy it for you. I have been carrying it around with me all of these years. I just had a feeling not to throw it away every time I was de-junking." His smile widens, "Do you like it?"

Tears are rolling down my cheeks as I nod my head yes, "I love it even more because you have kept it. You knew, just like I did, that we would see each other again." I put down the tiniest doll and without thinking of all the maybes and shouldn'ts and mights, wrap my arms around his neck and kiss him. It was not a soft, gentle kiss, it was a heavy, pressured kiss. My lips burned and my teeth threatened to pierce through the back of my lips, but I continued to kiss him. I felt his hesitation for only a second and then he responded with as much force as my own. We fervently ran our fingers up and down one another's backs and through each other's hair. My clip was pulled loose and my hair cascaded around my shoulders, he pulled back and looked at me, "I like it," he said coolly, and then kissed me again. My face was red and hot with passion and I could feel his skin moistening beneath his shirt and I ended the kiss.

"I," I said coyly, "have something for you as well!" I knew I was taking a risk by stopping, I should just power through, he was in the zone and cooler heads were not going to prevail. But I felt, as I did in that car that night, if it was going to happen, I wanted it to be real. This was a risk I had to take and a risk I hoped I wouldn't regret for the rest of my life.

I stepped away into the closet and brought out a silver cookie tin and offered it to him in much the same way he had given me the box. He smiled and opened it. Inside, his eyes confusedly studied the objects: a sandstone with a Kokopelli carved in it, a Beanie Baby Mountain Goat, a postcard of Mt. Rushmore, and a puzzle box. He turned the puzzle box over and over between his fingers and rattled it next to his ear. Two minutes later he tapped it lightly on the edge of the nightstand and the lid slid away. We both smiled eagerly. Inside a silver tissue paper awaited his unwrapping to finally reveal a silver chain necklace with an OHM pendant attached.

"It is beautiful," he said.

"I got it for you when I was in Nepal studying with the Tibetan Monks." I pause, not sure if I should go on, but the sparkle in his smile urges me forward, "I always remember you talking to me about the Buddhist culture and saying you'd like to learn more about the Dalai Lama's writing one day. When an internship opened up, I felt like I owed it to you, somehow, to go." I didn't know how to explain myself further and I was happy that he didn't ask any questions but simply kissed me again. This time, it was much calmer, more purposeful, each movement was thought out and tested. This wasn't the heat of the moment, this was something rehearsed, remembered, something longed for and missed.

Finally, he hit the bottom of the box and brought out a book of postcards held together by silver binder clips, the top read: TRAVELING WITH YOU IN MY HEART in cursive, silver letters with a picture of deep space behind it. He slowly began to turn the pages one by one, first looking at the picture, then the writing on the back. Munich, Paris, Rome, Toronto, Minneapolis, Oklahoma City, the alien concrete sculpture in the Salt Flats... he looked at each one. I had bought him a postcard every place I had been in the last ten years. I would like to say it was sixteen, since I last saw him, but it wasn't until a few years after that night in the car that I knew I would see him again. As clearly as I knew my own name and what I wanted from this life, I knew his part in it was not over. Each postcard I would write the same thing, the place, the date, and what made me think of him. Sometimes it was something as simple as a buffalo or prairie dog and sometimes it was something more profound like seeing a little part of him in every person, somewhere he had lived, somewhere I knew he had been, somewhere that we went together, or somewhere I knew he would love, like Nepal. Carefully, he looked at each one and said quietly, "There must be at least a hundred here…" he shook his head with confusion and disbelief.

"One hundred and eight," I respond and place a gentle hand on his knee.

Zeke moves the papers and gifts off the bed, slowly, carefully and clicks the lamp next to the bed off. I feel his hands beneath my dress and I instinctively move with them. I feel his breath on my neck and taste his sweat on my lips. He caresses me slowly and responds as I move my hand up and down his back and down his thighs. His fingers are entangled in my hair and I gasp as he pushes inside of me. I hold my breath and try to relax, to soak it all in, to remember every second. But as he rocks, I began to feel light headed, the room begins to narrow and I see stars and I smile and say, "I can see stars!" "and that, my dear, is why you are my star," "he replies with an extra thrust of his pelvis pushing him still deeper into me.

"So," Zeke began quietly as I lay curled up next to him, shoulder under his armpit and my leg lying across both of his. "What you been up to?" He laughed as he said it and kissed the top of my head. I smile and curl in deeper, breathing in the familiar scent that hasn't ever really left my nostrils.

"Not much really. I have been teaching, writing, and teaching some more." There were so many things I wanted to tell him. So many times over the years that I had tried to set up a casual meet and see him again, so many times I heard or saw something that reminded me of him. There was a whole world of me that I wanted him to see, that I knew he would like, that I hoped would make up for all the rest. I want him to understand me now. Now, without all the blurring of who I am versus whom I thought I wanted to be. But in all that, I knew that there was no telling that, so I bite my lip slightly and wait for his reply.

"Teaching, huh? That really suits you." Startled by his response I look up to see if there is any hint of joking in his eyes; there isn't and then I remember, I haven't talked to him, I mean really talked to him since just after I graduated with my Bachelor's degree.

"Oh… I forget I haven't talked to you in a long, long time." I smile and blush at the assumption that he has kept tabs on me and my life as I have with him. I knew when he moved, when he moved back, when he got married, when his son was born, when his wife was sick. I sent cards and well-wishing emails for each of the large events in his life. Twice a year or so, for the past twelve years, I have sent him a card on his birthday or Christmas, never both, and an occasional email. I thought I had told him things about my career and my life, but there was never any guarantee that he had read them, and he had only responded a handful of times. "I have a double PhD in Education and in the Psychology of Reading and Writing. I have been teaching at the University for nearly eight years and also teach adjunct classes at a few colleges around the area. Not so much for the money as for the ability to teach different areas and different levels of students. I want to expose as many students as possible to the thrills and advances in education!"

I can tell I am getting excited and speaking louder than the situation dictates. I take a deep breath and speak more calmly and quietly, "I have written two textbooks and am in the process of writing a third." I pause and feel him nod his head, but say nothing, so I go on, "Well, as you know, the last time we spoke, I had just graduated with my BA in English Literature and when you said no, I then moved to San Francisco and got my MA in Writing and then I moved to Minnesota and got my first doctorate in Education. I worked as a classroom teacher for a few years, but felt my ideas were being stifled in the districts, so I moved back to Salt Lake and graduated from the U with my emphasis in Psychology of Reading and Writing and have been guiding teachers to be better at their craft ever since." I pause and add, "And you?"

I already know all the promotions and moves he has taken for his career, but it is the polite thing to do, ask. He just says, "Same old, same old." And leaves it at that. We lay there silently, nodding in and out of sleep for a few hours when I feel him beginning to pull away. I take another deep breath, knowing this had to come and to not fight it, I have been given more than I deserve or even hoped to expect. I smile, hopefully, sweetly and tell him it is OK and that I understand. He gets dressed slowly and quietly in the dark. I can just make out his shadow and his movements are so familiar, the bowing of his head, the way he puts one arm through his shirt before his head and the second one seems to just appear on the other side of the sleeve. How his hands move when he ties his shoes and buckles his belt. It is so funny how little a person really changes and still, how vastly different they are. I know that I am smiling, I am happy and am trying to remember these final moments.

He comes and sits next to me on the bed and checks his phone for the time. He caresses my hair gently and whispers something into the top of my head. "What?" I ask. "Nothing. I was just thanking you for having the courage to come here today." He pauses and I smile, "I have thought about it many times, when

I have been in town. But I just couldn't ever call you."
He rubs the side of my arm as he speaks and I relax on
his clothed chest again.

"You never had anything to prove to me, ya
know…" he said allowing his sentence to trail off.

"What?!" I asked a little accusatorily.

"I mean, I have always known how beautiful,
smart, gifted, and spiritual a person you are. You
didn't have to get eight masters and ten doctorates to
show me, or anyone else, how wonderful you are." He
jostles my shoulder jokingly and I relax, a little.

"I don't' have eighteen 8 degrees." I answer.

"Close enough. You were always good enough.
You were always interesting enough. You were always
enough." He lifts my chin and kisses me softly and
finally.

"And…" I answer in a whisper, "because of you, I
always believed I was and that I could do anything." I
kiss him back and as I pull away I add, "Thank you."

One last kiss on the top of my head and he is at the
door, he turns around, waves a cute little wave that
won't allow me to believe that one day has passed and
he walks out of the door closing it softly behind him.

I awake early and pack my clothing methodically.
I have packed and unpacked this suitcase so many
times that I know where each item should be placed to
make it zip up perfectly. Checking out of my room I
ask the front desk clerk for the best place in all of town

for breakfast. I am not surprised when she answers, "Fynn's."

Fynn's has been around since my grandpa was a boy and they serve only breakfast and only on Thursday, Friday, and Saturday. They have four or five menu items that change and there are no substitutions and you have to be a long-standing local customer to be allowed to order off the menu. The lines are usually down the block, but a single can usually sneak in. I automatically drive to the small, white building that looks more like a house than a restaurant and notice that the patio is still fairly empty and the heat hasn't begun to sear the ground yet. I tell the host one and he leads me to the patio and hands me the piece of printer paper that has today's menu simply typed on it, clearly from a computer in the backroom. I order juice and Eggs Benedict and pull out my journal and begin to write about all the events of the last two days. I will be driving home today, straight through, no stopping for anything but gas and to pee.

Waiting for my food and pausing to recollect on every detail of last night, I look up and see a VW Bug pulling into the parking lot with South Dakota plates and my heart begins to beat faster. I take a deep breath and take a drink of water and stare at the plate, "It is crazy!" I say to myself, "but I guess of all times…" I trail off remembering that I am in public and talking aloud to myself.

But I guess of all times, I think this time, now is the most opportune. I was twenty-two and deeply concerned with everything: the state of the world, the state of my body, the state of my brain, the state of my soul. I was not comfortable with any part of myself and that meant not comfortable with any part of anyone else. Everyone and everything was a fix-it project. People were something I could help, things were something I could fix, my life revolved around trying to fix myself by trying to fix everything else. The problem, as problems always are, was that my model for "fix" was a bit skewed. But I couldn't know that yet, I was twenty-two and knew everything. In all of my life, I can remember exactly the first time when all that swirling just stopped. When who needs this and what is next and what should I do, say, think, wear, eat, act and how can I get everyone around me to match whatever I am doing, saying, thinking, wearing, eating, acting without everything becoming redundant all just stopped. There was nothing in my head or on my lips and my heart swelled with warmth and I felt perfectly, still. I was peaceful and happy and just, still.

Zeke's parents lived in the Badland's National Park and we went to visit them that second summer we were together. I wasn't nervous about meeting his family, because I was sure that Zeke and I were a healing relationship that wouldn't last. I was still under the impression that you needed to be educated to be smart and be ambitious to be happy, and he was neither. We drove around the huge, deserted park in places others were not allowed to go. We hiked, we picked wildflowers, we went to a dinosaur bone dig, we were attacked by buffalo, we ate fudge and ice cream at Wall Drug, we took pictures on the thirty-foot Prairie Dog and waded in fields of sunflowers. The Badlands were a magical place that took all thought away and everyone is allowed to live in the moment. Every kiss, every hug, every touch there was the cleanest, deepest, and most meaningful that I have ever experienced, even since.

One night, we built a huge bonfire and were making S'mores and laughing and telling stories and I happened to look over at Zeke and realized that this was the first time that I was actually seeing him, the full him. I smiled genuinely lovingly at him and he leaned over and kissed me very carefully, very gently as if not to break me, to not break this. I knew that us being here was different than it ever had been at home. I resisted the urge to over-analyze and talk it out. Was it him that was different, was it me, was it that I had just never bothered to really look at him at home, was I not able to be the real, pure me at home because of all the baggage and memories there, was he a man without baggage and so he could be pure here? I kissed him back, ferociously and whispered, "Let's go back." We stood up and without the need for goodbyes or excuses we merely put our roasters down and waved goodbye. No moans or pleads to stay, we just wordlessly walked away. The silence continued back to the house and into our bedroom, his childhood room had been remodeled into a fancier, more sophisticated guest room. He had told me where his He-Man poster and his model airplanes and helicopters had been our first night here. Now, it felt like a Victorian room with deep greens and browns and flowers and velvets. We lay on the bed and he undressed me, still silent and without a kiss. Kissing had always been an integral part of our foreplay and my mouth ached for him to kiss it, but he didn't. He ran his finger down my spine and across my butt until I got goosebumps and then he turned me over and caressed my stomach and upper thighs in the same manner. He rubbed his lips, gently, up and down each arm, never fully kissing or pulling away. Zeke slowly undressed and lay effortlessly beside me. I turned over towards him and cradled myself in the crook of his arm and breathed him in. We sat there for several minutes until I couldn't take the stillness any longer and straddled him and kissed him as hard as I could on the mouth and the world began to darken and I could see my vision narrowing, I rolled over to my back and pulled him into me as his face became more and more distant. I moaned without thought, a carnal, instinctive moan and he responded. My head became more and more dizzy and finally I stopped and cried out, "All I can see is stars!" he kissed me and continued.

Lying next to one another, he smiled and said, "We finally have a nickname for you! My Star."

"I can't be everyone's star…" I whispered quietly, afraid to break the silence.

"To everyone else, you will just be Star… but you will always be 'My Star'." He kissed the top of my forehead and we both drifted off into blissful sleep.

I have often thought about going back to South Dakota, but I have never been quite able to do it. Was there magic there without Zeke? Was that my one and only time to experience such delights? I liked to believe that it was magical, and if I ever do go back, I will be able to just be still again… I like having that place, that nirvana of one day I can go back there and simply be still.

I realize that I am crying, just a little, and I try and pull myself together.

"I have been chasing the peace ever since…" I say aloud and quickly add, to myself, I have a long journey home and it won't do anyone any good for me to be blubbering and re-licking old wounds again and again. I finish my breakfast, scratch off a quick note and tear the paper from my journal and leave. Placing the note on the windshield of the car, I smile and head off to pick up my car at the car rental place.

I think of the lines I wrote and feel like it has all come full circle:

You live in the most magical state in the universe!! Have a great day and get back there soon!
❤

Suddenly, he pulled away and turned on the ceiling light. "I want to see you, every part of you," he whispered as he pulled my dress up over my head, he released my hair from my ponytail and slipped my panties down my legs so effortlessly I almost didn't notice. He caressed me, slowly, looking over, inspecting, memorizing every inch of my body. I squirmed a little under his gaze, thinking about my thick ankles, the stretch marks on my thighs, the paunch of my belly, the galaxy of moles on my back, but with each kiss, each touch, I grew more and more comfortable with his eyes on me. As he moved his hands, his lips, his eyes from place to place, he made up little stories about how each part was made in magic and gifted to me, for him to behold, by some mystical being. My moles were pause marks from the pencil of Hemmingway, my light skin porcelain cast by Michelangelo, the visible veins maps to my heart by Lewis & Clark, the rising blush in my skin as the touch flush of Marie Antoinette. Touching my skin lightly with the tip of his finger, he spoke gently, sweetly and lightly kissed me over and over. My need for darkness disappearing and my need for him growing.

As I enter the freeway heading East, which will take me both North and East to home, I shake my head. It was only over a week ago that none of this had happened. None of this had even crossed my mind. I was living my everyday life: getting up, making breakfast, working, cleaning, doing laundry, and trying to remember to exercise; but now, it was all as if I had been planning it for years, as if I knew that one day I would spend an entire marvelous week in my past and would sew up all those old wounds. Say the goodbyes the way I wished I would have before. Take the memories of the last time I saw their face with me, locked down to never forget. I hadn't realized that those moments were so precious before, and have spent nearly two decades with regret and apologies on the tip of my tongue. Just one more stop I tell myself. I will drive up the canyon and sit in that perfect spot where the rocks are red in one direction, white in the other, jet black in another, and a pale yellow in yet another and finish this journey, properly.

The hike was longer and hotter in the July heat than I had remembered and I hoped the large Nalgene bottle of water would be enough. I had a huge Ikea rainbow umbrella to create a little shade, but the heat would just have to be endured, this was the spot of my childhood. My dad would bring us here on picnics and show us the exact right spot to see all of the colors of the diverse Utah rocks. I would come here in my teen years when I needed to think, I had brought Zeke, Jon, and Brick here at some point during our courtships. I always thought I would get married standing in this spot, or at least engaged. But none of that mattered, this was the nearest place to a holy site that I knew of and my writing would be completed here. I had finished off with Zeke's story earlier at the café and now, I open the book slowly to the front pages I had left blank, it was time to begin this story.

Day 7
September 3

People are weak.

So many of us are born with more weaknesses than strengths. Things that build walls around us and won't let us out to become who we could become, who we should become. It isn't our faults that as small children these things are placed heavily on our shoulders and we don't know what to do with them. Maybe if you are laid with one or two stressors, you can take a step back and see how silly and manageable they are… Maybe you can even start to unload them. But most of us aren't shouldered with a few, but dozens. Insecurities that shadow your everyday living: are you smart enough, funny enough, cute enough, skinny enough, talented enough, coordinated enough, calm enough, energetic enough, eloquent enough, aggressive enough, confident enough? How can a small mind suffer the pains of so many questions and second guessing? Many don't and those that do, it takes years and years and countless mistakes and missteps and regrets to unburden yourself one by one.

I awoke on July 7th and as I stumbled to the bathroom and as I stood a scent so foreign to me that I had to sit back down, I knew I was changed. It took only moments for my mind to piece all of the parts together and then, to know what I must do.

Your father may be one man, one man that I don't really know. Don't really know what I am giving to you. One man that I met and slept with one night in haste, as I am sure you will grow up and do too, my darling daughter, but I made sure that you were marinated in the essence of the greatest men I have ever known. Each of them helped me unburden myself of silly insecurities and ideals that weren't really part of who I was. Each of them have magical gifts and I wanted each of them to be your father, at one time, and yes, even now. Through them, I am releasing these burdens, these curses of birth from you and giving you a lighter load. Giving you, my precious, a chance to live from the beginning.

Please do not fall back into the trappings as I fear the shadow of the insecure will still remain, but be strong and know that you have a gift from each of them, that little specks of them seeped in as you divided and split and you are part of them all and they have released you as they did me.

I love you,
Mom